BURNS BOY

Praise for Krupa Ge's *What We Know About Her*

Longlisted for the JCB Prize for Literature 2021

Shortlisted for the inaugural Women Writer's Prize

'Krupa Ge was born to write and pin readers to the page. Her writing has spirit, presence, kickassery you want to bottle and snort. Few write about cities, people and fallibilities as well as she does.'

– Deepak Unnikrishnan, author of *Temporary People*

'A graceful, complex and heartbreaking work about how the past shelters and unmoors us. Krupa Ge writes like a dream.'

– Supriya Nair, writer and editor

'Steeped in memory, social commentary, curiosity, and Carnatic music Krupa Ge's *What We Know About Her* is a fiction debut to be cherished.'

– Hansda Sowvendra Shekhar, *National Herald*

'Her debut novel is also charged by her confident storytelling, along with her ability to illuminate the intersections of caste, class and gender, especially in the lives of people who are loathe to reckon with these uncomfortable truths.'

– Somak Ghoshal, *Mint Lounge*

'When I think of how my life will be chronicled by future generations ... I hope that the women in my life are not painted as victims, but in the rich shades Krupa Ge affords to her characters.'

– Gayathri Sankar, *Scroll.in*

'What Krupa Ge has achieved in her debut novel *What We Know About Her* is a depiction of reality without boundaries ... Yet, if you were to ask what the book is about the unequivocal answer would be, "women". The novel is a tender depiction of Indian women and their agency.'

– Percy Bharucha, *Hindustan Times*

'... unputdownable. I finished the book so fast, like I was devouring a tasty burger, one big bite after another ... The story moves like a gently flowing river, aided by the cool breeze of Ge's writing.'

– Rachna Chhabria, *The Asian Age*

'Krupa Ge's debut novel is about making journeys. The journey of unravelling the truth, the journey is in time too, from the past to the present and back, especially through the letters written by the protagonist—Yamuna's grandmother to her grandfather. It is a journey even in terms of geography, particularly between the two cities which have their own character in the novel—Chennai and Banaras. She depicts the journey of the struggles of the women ... belonging to three generations ... Consequently, it also becomes a journey of the self.'

– Jennifer Monteiro, *The Book Review*

BURNS BOY

KRUPA GE

Published by Context, an imprint of Westland Books, a division of Nasadiya Technologies Private Limited, in 2025

No. 269/2B, First Floor, 'Irai Arul', Vimalraj Street, Nethaji Nagar, Alapakkam Main Road, Maduravoyal, Chennai 600095

Westland, the Westland logo, Context and the Context logo are the trademarks of Nasadiya Technologies Private Limited, or its affiliates.

ISBN: 9789360451936

10 9 8 7 6 5 4 3 2 1

This is a work of fiction. Names, characters, organisations, places, events and incidents are either products of the author's imagination or used fictitiously.

Typeset by Jojy Philip

Printed at Thomson Press (India) Ltd

For Ninaad

1

Then

A boy in a burns ward is a thing of pity.

On the day of the explosion, I was a living corpse, running, howling. Then I heard Amma scream, a blood-curdling scream that outdid my own. When she ran towards me and ripped open my burning shirt, peeling it off my body, I felt my skin, already singed, tear and come off along with the shirt like Velcro in little girls' shoes. Then there was only pain. As I was losing consciousness, I sensed it, the burning on my nerves and my skin, like a million, no, ten million, maybe a hundred million pinpricks all at once, on my arm, my shoulder, deep inside my head.

First there was that saucepan. Old, worn, like all things in that kitchen, the oldness, dullness, wornness that lent them comfort, made them seem blameless. The scratches, its lightness, its dimples, all added to the aluminium pan's innocent aura. I wouldn't even be thinking about it now, or ever, if it weren't for that day. When water boiled over and I absent-mindedly gripped its scraggy, uncovered arm. And it was all heat—unbearable, angry. As if I were inside the pan itself.

Why did I touch the handle? My mother had instructed me to turn the stove off, no more. I had seen the grown-ups on TV move pans away from stovetops; I had seen my own mother do it. My mother handled the pan, I remembered later, with the end of her sari. I learned a lesson in conduction that day.

By the time I finally realised what I had done and let go of the wretched handle, the pan tipped over and the red-hot water in it splashed. Steam landed on parts of my palm I'd never paid attention to until then. Then the pan tipped over, emptying its contents onto my palm, and my little gasps finally took the form of a scream that could be heard across the neighbourhood.

At this point my mother, instead of rushing over, simply called out to me from the other room, asking me in that irate, vexed tone of hers—what is it now? I continued to scream, tears blurring my vision, brain unable to comprehend the scalding, feeling a sort of emptiness I hadn't felt ever before, but the pain reminding me that I was still alive.

I wished I'd fainted then, that I could reach into my brain and stop it from functioning. Even later, as the numbing cream wore off or the painkiller began to reach the end of its effectiveness, that dreadful feeling returned, and I thought I would actually die.

I didn't.

I was alive. With pain.

We were not modern enough to own those vessels, ones that you could touch right away. We could afford them, sure, but just because you could afford something, you didn't buy it, not in my house. There must be a need. After that day, though, we finally got a stainless steel, copper bottom milk pan with a black plastic handle screwed on to it.

Something about her that day was disappointing, my mother, I mean. I couldn't figure out what. Something happened that day that neither she nor I could undo.

After the accident, though, things returned to calm for a while. Every day, she took me to a lab nearby to have the blisters on my palm burst. They had grown enormous. For days, the two of us walked from home to the lab and back. Now that I think about it, those walks were nice. We were mostly quiet. My mother wrapped up in her thoughts, writing in the air, her fingers always moving. Sometimes she'd even strike something she wrote and then try to rewrite. I gave up trying to figure out what she was writing, it was too fast.

Those days, she looked thinner than ever in her Garden Vareli sarees, printed with bold flowers all across, and she looked tall, which she wasn't exactly, it was the synthetic sarees that made her seem so. She wore a faint lip colour that nobody could make out, except us, her kids, and her watch was always on her right wrist, the strap on the front of her arm, and the dial at the back, parallel to her palm. So, whenever she had to tell time, she flicked her wrist, her fingers folded neatly into her palm. Only when we had to cross the road at a big junction did she hold me. Even then she made it look like she needed my support to cross the road. She was great at helping everyone around her keep up appearances, my mother.

My hand, misshapen with giant blisters that looked like smooth pebbles, was as disgusting to me as it was a strange source of wonder. I nearly ran out of the lab the first time the assistant told me he was going to have a go at them with a pin. A pin, of all things! My mother held my other hand, and the assistant told me to look away. How could I look away? I looked right at him, at the pin, at my gaunt arm. This won't hurt at all, he promised. It didn't. I began to enjoy the feeling of release and then I felt envious of the lab assistant. My body was producing water balloons and someone else was having fun bursting them? At home, I did the pin-poking to smaller blisters even though he warned me not to do it.

When the large, small and tiny blisters all finally went away, my palm and the back of my hand were both the exact same colour, white as chalk, with a touch of pink, unsettling. I could slowly use that arm then, but all my friends kept a safe distance from it, and me, as I umpired through the summer I turned twelve. No batting, bowling, fielding or keeping. I tried to bat with the other hand for a while, then gave up on cricket.

That was my first real encounter with heat. With burns. Now it seems so trivial as I lie here all burned for the second time, and this time it isn't just my palm. And this time, it isn't just some blisters.

I am the only boy here in a ward full of women with extremely serious burns. Gas cylinder burns, dowry burns, love failure burns, jilted-lover-pours-kerosene burns. The stuff you read about in the news. Since it's not Diwali now, not even close, there aren't any other kids who got adventurous and / or unlucky with firecrackers in this ward. They are still shocked I am here.

I heard my mother tell the nurses, who had all taken to calling me 'that burns boy', since I was the only boy in the ward the day I was admitted, about the elaborate April Fool's prank I had pulled on my neighbours when it was still December. So, this too is expected of him, she was telling them. Back in December, she had me write a formal apology, in triplicate, like she was going to have it notarised. I had to write a letter saying I would never write letters again.

This letter trouble, as all troubles of mine that season, began with boredom. The slowness of that morning weighed us down like it was a real, physical thing. It was the first morning of the Christmas holidays, I was with my friend Lakshmi, and we were both already bored. I told her I had a great idea. I really did, I promised when she looked unconvinced.

Okay, so I was in the mood to do something—something funny, even if it was not brilliant. She followed me around quietly, because I was kind of the ringmaster of the building and a year older than her. I was the one to first explain to her when we were still in primary school what all the bad words her mother used meant. Fuck means a man and a woman lie in bed without any clothes. Then their private parts meet. Bitch? That's just a female dog. Why is that a bad word? It just sucks to be a she dog. Then bastard? That's me. She laughed so hard then. So, you can see why she gave me the benefit of the doubt when I said I had a funny idea. I went home and picked up an unused blue inland letter and my mother's jotter pen, and then quietly slipped out. We looked for a shaded spot. I stood beside the pillion seat of my neighbour's dirty blue Chetak, and Lakshmi sat on the driver's seat. I placed the letter on the seat and began to write, carefully controlling my handwriting because it was an unruled page. I poked a few holes in the sheet and the scooter seat with the pen. But the words, they just came to me, I didn't even have to think. I wrote to lovely Smita aunty from upstairs—she gave me incredible food, involved me in her life, and treated me like a son—that I had kidnapped her husband, and that if she wanted to see him alive, she must come with one lakh rupees in a green suitcase to Vandaloor Zoo. And that if she went to the police, she would never see him again, ever. I wrote her name and address under the 'To' column in front, and in the back, I wrote, 'From, Forest Brigand Sandalwood Smuggler Veerappan, Karnataka'. Then I stuck a used stamp from an insurance letter lying around in my house and dropped it off in the building's common box from where everyone picked up their mail.

Smita aunty, who moved to the building a year ago, had unexpectedly befriended me. In the evenings, she gave me carrot halwa, biscuits or cream buns, and on festival days she always sent something special for me, me alone. Smita aunty was so light-skinned that she frightened me a bit initially. I had never seen someone that colour. Everyone in my life was properly brown. And she was only the second woman I knew who had silky brown hair; the other was a neighbour who dyed her grey hair with henna. Smita aunty spoke only Hindi and English, she wore beautiful clothes and a really big bindi in red. The things I remember the most about her though are that her smile was all teeth and gums, that she was very affectionate to me, that she had actually decorated her home and walls. Posh bed sheets, curtains, wall hangings. We used rough practical sheets that my mother bought years ago for cheap from a handloom cooperative that gave discounts to government employees, that's where the curtains were from too, and our walls were for calendars and bags of all shapes. Smita aunty also dressed very differently, not at all like any of us in that building. She was like the women in the arty, boring Hindi movies Amma watched on Doordarshan on Sundays. Her handsome musician husband was the object of our admiration. Us boys, we were dazzled by his sunglasses and hair, and the girls, they seemed to love everything about him. That I was close to this happening couple added to my ringmaster status, obviously.

After I dumped the letter in the box, I expected the watchman—whose job it was to collect the mail from the postman and drop it in the common post box in the building—to figure out right away that there was a fake letter in there. I figured he might even get a laugh out of it and throw it in the dustbin. If I, a school kid, knew it was fake, he, a full-grown man, would know too, how could he not? Or, if he failed to notice it, Smita aunty or her husband would laugh with me about it over tea and ajwain rusk the following Sunday afternoon. But then nothing at all happened, and I forgot about it and moved on to other worries, like more pimples and bad scores, until I returned from school one day to find my mother standing at the gate to our building, holding my orange ruler, huffing menacingly, like that cheetah I'd seen on National Geographic.

This was two whole weeks after I posted that letter. She had waited for me at the bus stop, she said. And watched me slowly amble down, taking the longer route home, kicking loose stones on the road. She lost patience and came back home ahead of me, taking the shorter route.

My mother then fed me lunch, all the while threatening to finish me off. I grew anxious and felt like I might vomit, but she snarled every time I tried to get up from the chair. To my frustrated questions about just what she was upset about, and what I had done, she only grasped the ruler harder and said, I will tell you after you eat. I swallowed four morsels of rice and ran to the bathroom. I racked my brains for half an hour inside the toilet, but couldn't figure out what I had done to enrage her so.

Neither she nor Smita aunty believed me when I said it was an April Fool's prank. They kept looking for reasons, asking me if I had some kind of vendetta against Smita aunty or her handsome husband. I tried to explain that I, in fact, liked her, which was why I thought she would get my joke. I found it incredible that they were making such a big deal of this.

When Smita aunty finally left the building a year later, she left a card for me with my mother. My mother gave it to me as soon as I came home from school. It was an innocent-looking generic fare well card with a preprinted message. She had just signed her initials at the bottom, I didn't read much into it. I was glad to receive it though because she'd stopped talking to me after the letter. My mother couldn't stand my nonchalance, how unaffected I was by this whole thing. Her voice dripping with sarcasm, her face twisted in contempt for me and Smita aunty, she'd asked, 'Don't you get it?'

'What?'

'What's on the card's cover?'

It was a woman and a man in a zoo. It was green-coloured, and joyous, there was a giraffe too.

'You don't get why they gave you this card, do you?'

To say goodbye, obviously.

'That card says, you are a little delinquent; it says you wrote a letter asking them to come to the zoo, threatening them for money . . . ' Then she muttered under her breath, 'Wait till I call your dad.'

I tore the card up, threw it in the dustbin and wept myself to sleep that night.

Everything before the burning, though, all these events and all emotions, felt to my fifteen-year-old self like child's play. What kept me up after that day was the stench of my shirt burning, and with it, my skin.

My mother lived her life avoiding even the shadow of offence. She made me lower the TV volume so we did not disturb the neighbourhood's peace, lectured me on keeping my voice to a whisper as if our guests (a permanent fixture in those years) might die if they heard me and not of whatever ailment they were here to be treated for. So I was baffled by how reckless she was when it came to me. From the second she ripped my burning shirt and my skin off my body, all of my fear and anger towards my own self and the fire I had lit was somehow redirected at my mother. I was very, very tired, but I remembered to stay angry.

That weekend when my mother suddenly decided to clean the loft shelves, a treasure I had to otherwise wait months for became unexpectedly available to me. Leftover firecrackers from Deepavali. I told my mother I would take care of them. I moved them to the backyard, and spent a whole day drying the dampness out of them all. The chakras, the sparklers, the flower pots, the bijlis and the Lakshmis, some meant for light, others for sound, or smoke, and my favourite, the black pellets that expanded into a snake-like black, vicious mass in a plume of smoke.

They were all laid out on newspapers, individually wrapped in newspaper, and made crisp under the sun. Since it was not Deepavali, I felt like I had to treat these firecrackers differently. I was not going to burst them as I would usually, one by one. So, after lunch, that day, I sat in the sun and opened every single cracker and took out the powder inside.

Soon my hands, legs, the ground, everything around me was covered in that glorious black, silvery powder, and that smell, ah, that new smell. Not like kerosene. Not like petrol. Something else. Something equally good. Maybe even better. I had to keep rubbing my hands clean on my shirt because it was getting a bit too wet with sweat and I didn't want to dampen my recently dried powder. Before I knew it, my shirt had turned almost entirely black near my left shoulder. It was an old shirt with holes, so my mother wouldn't mind. She would tear it in two, in that way of hers, with a totally satisfied face, and use it to wipe things. I made a neat little parcel of all the powder from the firecrackers in a newspaper, slinked into the kitchen and got the matchbox out. My mother was having coffee in there, flirting incorrigibly with some guest, my father's friend, I think. I saw him for the first time that day, but it didn't matter to me who he was. She was overly friendly with everyone but her children. I made a face when neither of them looked, then ran out and was distracted by my firecrackers.

On the way out, I took my glasses off, and kept them safe above the TV in the living room. I was worried about dropping them while playing. I washed my hands clean with Amma's Mysore Sandal soap in the backyard. Then I dried it on my shirt. I carefully positioned the parcel away from my body, and then I walked around it to see how it looked from all directions. Once I was satisfied with my work of art, I squatted down and struck the match. I lit the edge of the paper, threw the matchstick down, and prepared to run. But it was already too late.

Deafening noise.

Incredible fire.

Me inside of it.

My shirt had caught fire, burning more brightly than the rest of my body. My sister Aparna, watching me from across the yard, stood unblinking. Her eyes fixed on me in horror, her hands up in the air like someone was about to shoot her. My mother said she had difficulty opening the old kitchen door. I had asked Aparna to just close it to keep my mother from coming out and seeing me playing with the firecrackers. My mother insisted for years that she had broken the door down in under a minute, but I could swear it was an hour. After she ripped my shirt off, Amma wrapped me in a woollen blanket, picked me up in her arms and ran out to the bus stop to catch an autorickshaw. She didn't wait for an auto. She kept running, that friend of hers, the one with whom she was busy gossiping while I was nearly dead, helped her carry me. Her wedding chain poked my wound, adding to the pain.

'I am going to die, just as you wished. Hope you're happy now,' I said as she ran breathlessly. She didn't say a thing back. She didn't pay attention to anything I said or did. I screamed and passed out by turns as she finally caught a rickshaw, and brought me to the burns ward.

When I opened my eyes the next morning, no one was around. There were people in the ward, just not around me. The room was calm, cool. My head was inside a cloud heavy with water. All this lasted just a few seconds, then from beyond all that fog, I felt the burning somewhere deep inside my body and soul. I thought I wasn't supposed to feel pain in the hospital, what use are doctors if they can't stop this? I couldn't find a way to move away from the wound. A pain that I never can explain to anyone in words, no matter how many languages I learn, was waiting patiently for me to wake up, and then all at once I was burning all over again, like I would melt any moment.

I didn't have my glasses, and so I couldn't even hide my tears. The world was still a blur, like that day I first figured out something was wrong. When I could no longer see match scores while lying on the sofa. Everyone else could. I wondered if the producers of the TV relay had changed the size of the score scroll suddenly. At the ophthalmologist's I couldn't believe they had to rely on me to tell them how well and if I could see. I thought it would be the other way round.

The thing I loved the most about not wearing glasses was how I looked better in the mirror somehow. I could not see the tiny imperfections that I hated, especially the acne. If I wanted to not feel so bad about my burns, I could just not wear my glasses while looking in the mirror. It might not be such a bad thing if my power increased. The less I could see, the better. I was glad I decided to give up on contact lenses then. After I accidentally slept with one on, I was sure they were just not worth it.

That overwhelming scent of kerosene from all the other burns patients, the smell of disinfectant, and what would come to be the familiar and soul-crushing stench of the dressing for burns survivors, all of it clung to the air, heavy like furniture in that sterile room. There was moaning, and tears. Much of it from the woman on the other side of my curtain, and her father.

My father was in Iraq. He would have to drop everything and rush home. I pictured him running through an airport, like in the movies. My mother must have packed my sister off to school, while she sat at home, writing. She loved pretending everything was normal. That's what kept her from feeling guilty for all the things she did.

Four nurses in green uniforms and cloth masks were helping the other patient out of her bed. She was making soft, animal noises. The nurses were very gentle with her, treating her like a baby. Whimpering, her legs fully plastered, she walked as if she really were a child learning to stumble. The nurses led her out of the ward to some place beyond the reach of my eyes. I was in a see-through tomb inside the plastic curtains that encircled my bed, and I now realised that I too was moaning with every exhalation, like an old man. How long had I been awake? There wasn't much else to watch, just the white interiors, blue sheets, in the distance a window. I tried not to think of my wound, not to lift my arm, not to touch the bandaged part. I succeeded for a while.

The IV needle and line, the first thing I remembered being plugged into as I entered the ward, was still connected. I wanted to be dignified, as my mother expected of me, I really did. But then I began to cry without really knowing why. At first, it too was a whimper like my neighbour's, like we were just two pups. Then it turned into gasps and then hisses, and before long, tears and heat. Two nurses rushed over. They knew that the source of my pain was in my heart as well, and they offered words, sweet, kind, comforting and loving.

'You are up, you brave boy.'

'Your mother was here all night, didn't sleep a wink. She just left.'

A boy in a burns ward is a thing of pity, I learned then.

I went to sleep again after medicines, and when I woke up I expected my mother to be by my bed. She wasn't. I felt a little pang, but ignored it. There were other things to worry about. Like school. And my impending death.

Bath and dressing done, my neighbour was on her way back in, and while I contemplated death, she was sobbing still. Two nurses stayed by her side to keep up her spirits for a while, and when it was time for tea, one of them came up to me and said, 'Will you please keep talking to her, dear? She needs company.' I nodded.

I waited for her to stop moaning. Only her legs were affected. If she wore a saree, or a churidar, or a long skirt, no one would even know. I looked at my hand then. The bandage was around my armpit and back and covered my arm until my elbow. I lost patience.

'Hi, I am Guru.'

She stopped moaning for a second, glared at me and then went back to moaning. I figured she was upset and decided to keep quiet. Then I went back to staring down at my own bandage. For some reason, the tears were back, and I was a pup again.

'How old are you?' she asked. Her voice was deep and soothing. I did not expect that, having only heard her high-pitched moans and cries.

'Does it hurt a lot?' I asked.

'What class are you in?' She was deflecting.

'Does it?' I repeated.

'I feel like it's better to die every time I go to bathe or to get the dressing.'

Was I supposed to feel like dying too?

'Nobody warned me about this, you know? You'll find out tomorrow anyway.'

I looked away to stop the tears. And then I swallowed my pride and said, 'Warn me.'

'Did it hurt when you took your clothes off after the burns?' she asked.

I nodded.

'Dressing feels like that. Only it's for longer.'

She looked at me all worried, then she tried to break into a smile, trying to erase what she had just said. She was feeling bad for me I could see.

'These sisters, they take such good care of us, no?'

I nodded. 'They asked me to keep you company.'

'You had a fireworks accident?'

I nodded. I wasn't sure if I should ask, but then I did anyway, 'Did someone hurt you?'

'You mean like for dowry,' she laughed, her eyes wide.

I just stared.

'No. I am not married. That's that lady in the room across ours. I am a chef. This happened at the restaurant I work in.'

'You are a chef?'

'I was hurt in the kitchen.'

'I don't want to ask you how it happened,' I said.

'Good.'

'What's your name?' I asked.

'Smita.'

Smita? The name came floating across the room, and then I couldn't say anything. Then she laughed and then coughed and laughed again.

'Did my mom tell you the Veerappan letter story when I was asleep?'

'My name is Seema actually,' she winked.

Did my mother think it was funny now? Or was it Seema that found it funny that I had written to Smita aunty pretending to be a forest brigand. Me, with that big, luscious moustache. Funny, funny, like it was meant to be? I could not figure out which of them I was supposed to credit with this, though.

'I am going to sleep for some time now. You should too,' she said.

Then I heard *her* enter the room, not a hair out of place, not looking even a bit worried. And again, totally involuntarily, tears began to roll out of my eyes, and I closed them, pretending to be asleep. I didn't open my eyes at all for what felt like an entire day. She knew even when her eyes were on the book she was reading, sitting next to my bed, that I was awake.

'Are you up?' she whispered.

I made sure to not close my eyelids too tight.

In my dream that night, I was a chef, planting sparklers inside a cake.

The next morning, I watched in horror as the quiet burns ward descended into utter chaos. At first, it looked like they were preparing for war, but quietly, efficiently. The resident doctors had been informed of a petrol tanker accident.

'It's going to be a busy day,' sister Ranjitha told me.

Even before the patients got to the ward, everything they would need had arrived. The wait was eerie. The horseshoe-shaped ward, where you had to make an effort to see what another patient was doing, began to slowly fill up, more and more, and then it was brimming over with burnt women, children and men. That smell would not be easily defeated, it was like we were in a petrol bunk. Twenty in all, the burn victims. Three kids were near my bed on stretchers.

The two resident doctors began with the first child. The woman doctor at the head of the child, poking the neck, the male doctor at the leg, poking around the ankle, looking for a spot to hook up the IV line on the child's singed skin.

After a painful couple of breaths, she yelled, 'Yes, got it,' and then he abandoned the leg, took his gloves off, wore new ones and moved to the next child. She hooked up the IV line to the first child, and joined him in poking the next child, and then the pained breathing continued. Again, she yelled, 'Yes, got it.' And he moved again, pulling on new gloves. With the next child, he found the spot right away; didn't say anything. He went about his job, and by the time he was done, two more breathless babies were wheeled in. The woman doctor called for help, her voice breaking.

'We need more hands here.'

In their rush to do paperwork for the new patients, the nurses had forgotten to draw the thick curtain over the plastic curtains across my bed. I could see everything the doctors were up to. I couldn't bear to keep looking, but I couldn't look away either. All of it felt like a skit they were putting on to show me the things I missed when I arrived, unconscious, at the hospital. If I felt fear, I didn't admit it to myself. I steeled my whole heart then, stopped every feeling. Before I went to sleep, I heard that some more people were brought in dead, and that some died immediately on arrival.

Things went back to being calm again in a few days. My mother came and went. I still wasn't talking to her. I was no longer angry, but I was sad, and always in pain. And I couldn't figure out what to say anymore. She had left a magazine by my bed. Her short stories appeared in many of those little Madras magazines. She wanted to write a novel, but just hadn't had the time to, she claimed. If she didn't spend so much time playing free nurse to every old or sick person in the family, she'd have written ten books.

I opened the Tamil magazine, and her face smiled back from inside the pages. 'My Tree' the article was called, and despite everything, I managed to smile.

'What are you smiling at?' Seema asked, her voice hoarse. The nurses said she smoked in the bathroom.

'There's this story my mother always tells me, about a tree she once saw. She has written about it for a magazine.'

'She was waiting around for a while, must have been to show you the piece.'

I stared at the magazine, pretending to have not heard Seema.

'Are you going to read it out for me?'

'I can just tell you the story I have heard it enough times.' I rolled my eyes.

'No, how will we kill time in this stupid place. You read your mother's article out to me first. Then I will read something else out for you.'

'I don't think I can hold the magazine for long with one hand,' I confessed.

'Ayyo. Shall I read it out to you then?' she perked up.

We waited for one of the sisters to come check in on us, and when sister Ranjitha finally did, she handed the magazine over to Seema and sat down to listen.

Seema opened the page with my mother's photograph and whistled. 'How good-looking is this woman?'

'Show me, show me,' Ranjitha squealed. I realised then that she must be young.

'See?' She held it up.

Smart. Sharp. Elegant. I heard the usual words people had for her.

'Okay,' Seema made some more grunting noises, this time like a goat giving birth, as she propped the magazine up and started to read 'My Tree'.

'How exciting,' Ranjitha said, squealing some more, 'You may have to translate for me wherever I can't understand formal Tamil.'

I nodded. Seema began reading without waiting for us to focus.

It really was the first time I felt anything close to love for a tree. It was so large and had many alcoves into which I wanted to lodge myself. And then the world would accept me, I too would be a part of the things it nurtured—moss, ferns and random small plants that had started to grow on its generous, handsome trunk. Its roots were so large I could climb on them and still feel stable. Everything about the tree screamed home. Whenever I saw it, I said, I love you, tree.

Even as I tried my best to focus on my mother's bizarre attraction to a tree, my mind kept wandering to school. To Nazia and Vinay. Did they know I was in the hospital? Were they going to use this chance to do all the things I'd been stopping them from doing? Would they visit? What might they feel for me, pity, disgust or love? Would Nazia finally dump Vinay and stay by my side and help me recover?

I imagined the school peon delivering the news of my death to the class teacher. The class teacher standing up in shock. Then, Nazia in my house, crying uncontrollably because of her love for me. I pictured her in my living room, I saw her hug me, and felt a certain thrill at first, and then an unspeakable sadness.

Nazia was my friend to begin with. Vinay sat next to me in class, and had his eyes on her. It was disgusting. I didn't want him to know how I felt, so I made friends with him too. We were not exclusive friends, we all had other things to do with our lives. But we got together a couple of times a week in the playground or outside, and exchanged plenty of gossip. We ate American chopsueys and pineapple cake at the newly opened Archana's Bakery down the road from school whenever we had money, but we didn't need the excuse of an outing to be with each other.

Vinay was a bit roly-poly, and I was reed thin. I wondered which was better in Nazia's eyes. Not for anything, just wondered which of us was better. At first. Soon I was thinking about it obsessively. The more I heard Vinay drool over Nazia, the more I began to see her differently. She was a bit pimply, like me, like most of us boys and girls. She was tall, averagely built. She wore a retainer now that her permanent braces were gone. She didn't stand out in any manner as far as I could see. Except when she smiled. There was definitely something about her smile. But because Vinay kept building her up all the time, I too began to imagine her as this unattainable girl. It was then that I began to find Vinay increasingly repulsive and ugly, a monkey who smelled of garbage. And she, beautiful, always fragrant and soothing, a mist of rose water. My face burned whenever I overheard them talk to each other, or when I found out they'd been talking on the phone over the weekend. The first time I heard it, I instinctively asked Nazia, 'How come you never call me?'

'I don't even have your number, da,' she said.

I wrote it down for her in her notebook. She smiled in an intimate manner that I really liked. And then I became even more confused about what was happening. Was I a friend, or did this jealousy mean something else? And in that confusion, I started something that I shouldn't have. When I was far away from school, in that hospital bed, far away from where I could control Vinay and Nazia, I worried they were going to fall for each other, and find out what I had done. Would I die a villain? I pictured them happy together, mad at me for fooling them, and then laughing at me, telling Eliamma Thomas, our Vice Principal whose favourite I was, just what I had done. My stomach began to hurt. And something like a lump was stuck in my throat. No matter how much water I drank, the lump never went away.

Frustrated and helpless as Vinay and Nazia grew closer, spending more and more time with each other, talking to each other all the time in class and outside, I began to lie to them.

I found myself one afternoon in the bathroom when a story began to come alive in my head. Once I was satisfied with all the details, I came back, looking worried and cross. When Nazia narrowed her eyes and nodded at me, gesturing with her thumb, what happened, I pointed to my watch and mouthed, wait, after the bell. I was sitting right next to Vinay. He wrote a question mark on my notebook.

I wrote, 'Met the VP.'

'Serious?'

I didn't say anything to him then.

I formed the sentences quietly in my head. I crossed my legs, folded my arms, and didn't look at either of them for the rest of Maths period. I knew they were making eyes at each other and laughing. Afterwards, slipping both my hands into my trouser pockets, I walked to the far end of the playground, where we parked our bicycles.

'What is it?' Nazia asked, her eyes wide with worry. Like she knew it was something ominous that involved her.

'Let's go sit in Archana's,' Vinay said, never one to miss a chance to sit with her.

I agreed.

'I am not coming,' Nazia protested.

'It's about you. And you,' I said, pointing to both of them.

They became very quiet. We pushed our cycles down Usman Road in jittery silence and entered the deserted bakery. I loved going to school by bus. I liked the feeling of untucking my white uniform shirt, unbuttoning it, so everyone could see the T-shirt I was wearing inside, standing on the footboard, and getting off at every stop to let people get off. Then when the bus started, I loved holding the black grab bar and running with the bus, jumping on to the footboard just in time. I could look at the girls who sat by the window. If I liked a girl, I gave her my bag. Then I looked at her and smiled once in a while. Most girls ignored me, but once or twice I got a smile back, and one girl even hugged my bag. I had to give up all of the thrill of the bus ever since Nazia and Vinay began cycling to school. I nagged my mother and fought with her until I had a better cycle than either of them.

As always, the air conditioning was on full blast at the bakery.

'Let's order first,' Vinay said, and I nodded. We were both acting like adults. Nazia was too worried to act.

After the waiter-cum-chef went into the kitchen to bring us our chop sueys and cakes, and it was just us in the bakery, I looked straight at them and lied.

'Eliamma has asked me to keep an eye on you both and report to her what you do.'

Nazia lowered her thus far wide-open eyes. Vinay opened his mouth to protest, then closed it. Then he found the words.

'Why would that stupid Vice Principal care about us?'

'She suspects you two are a thing, and she doesn't want any trouble from your parents, or worse, your communities.' I was improvising. *Divide et impera.* It was a lesson from our history books. Pit the Hindu against the Muslim. My words came out well formed.

'So? What does she want you to do?' Nazia asked feebly.

I glared at her. 'Aren't you upset that she's mistaken your friendship for something else?'

'We are best friends. We will talk to each other. What's it to anyone?' she was defiant.

Vinay looked utterly satisfied with himself, but also a bit worried. 'What should we do, da?' he asked, and then he put his slimy fingers on Nazia's index finger and tapped it gently to reassure her that he'd take care of it all.

'You're lucky I am the one she's asked this favour from,' I declared. 'Just make sure I am with you whenever you guys hang out and it will all be okay.'

'Thanks a lot, da,' he slapped my back, clapped his hands and winked at Nazia. I caught her blushing.

I spent the entire afternoon thinking of Nazia, and couldn't catch a nap. Later, when I was in the middle of an animated conversation with Seema, my mother walked in, my sister in tow. Aparna looked desolate, scared, but didn't hide behind my mother the way I had when she was admitted to the hospital with appendicitis. She was younger but acted older, and was definitely braver than me most times. She came up to me and smiled brightly.

Aparna had picked up some books from the library and brought some mints. 'I didn't know what you can eat, but these you can slip into your mouth when no one is around,' she said.

I caught my mother staring at Aparna, observing her as she would an object in a museum. I ignored her and kept talking to Aparna, showering her with more pointed affection to make up for my mother's scrutiny. Amma slipped across to Seema's bedside and laid two rotten old books there. Seema could barely conceal a shriek.

'Thank you, these are so rare, ya.' It was strange to hear her, my friend, talk to my mother like they were also friends.

Aparna turned around sharply and stared at the books in Seema's hands. She ran across from my bed and snatched them from Seema and brought them over to me.

'Couldn't you show him first, Amma, before giving it away?'

Amma didn't say anything. Whatever Aparna needed to hear would be delivered to her in the privacy of our home. Here, Amma was still the perfect lady, floral saree, hair in place, watch on her wrist, handbag on shoulders, skin spotless. When my grandmother said she looked like an airhostess—and in her book, my grandmother's that is, that was high praise—my mother had snapped back, 'A well-dressed caretaker you mean, that's what men want?'

I looked at the books in my hand. One of them looked literally like it had been snatched out of a pig's mouth. It had no cover, ends bitten, the paper was so brittle that it was breaking, not even tearing. *Cooking Made Simple* by Gertrude Wilkinson. Home Economist, Garden City, New York. 1962. The other was in better shape, even though it was older. *Jams, Jellies and Preserves: How to Make Them* by Ethelind Fearon. London: Herbert Jenkins. 1953. Inside, a seal read 'Rupayana Booksellers, Rampurawala Building, Indore City, Agents for Govt of India Publications'. My grandfather must have bought them on one of his trips.

I had zero interest in cookbooks. Once Aparna was convinced I didn't care for the books, she dropped them off by Seema's bed. Then she rushed back to me and told me about school in whispers. Nazia had called on the landline and my mother had told her I was in the hospital.

'Does she know which hospital?'

'Hmmm.'

'Is she going to visit?'

She shrugged.

That put me in a better mood. My mother was talking to Seema, but her eyes were on me and my sister. So, I lowered my voice too.

'If she calls again, tell her to come visit me after the surgery,' I said.

Aparna's face fell. 'You are going to have a surgery?'

'Didn't Amma tell you? They are going to take skin from my thighs and put it on my arm.'

'What?' it was her turn to whimper.

Then she ran out of the hospital room. She never visited me in hospital after that day. I was glad she reacted like that, because I had never shaken off the guilt of having been healthy, wolfing down cakes and Chinese food as Aparna lay in a hospital bed during her surgery. Even though I was smiling, my mother was still scowling at Aparna. When she saw me staring at her, she assumed a regular face, and then slowly tried to smile at me. I looked away. She had done this to me, she was why I needed the surgery. How could she sit there looking guiltless? My sister felt the guilt. How could my mother come there, showing off her unblemished face and arms to me, showing off her health so shamelessly? As all the anger I had pushed inside came back, I leaned on an old, reliable habit. One I had perfected as a child before I had the words for my anger. I took aim at the bed pan—no one except Seema and my mother could see what I was doing—and peed right there in front of them. I had threatened to do this countless times, in crowded spaces when I was scared, when I wanted to leave some place, when I felt suffocated by the mobs on Fridays in temples, and those long queues to meet oracles who read faces, palms, cowry shells, what have you, swamijis and gurujis, horoscope readers and numerologists, in that phase of hers when she believed in every voodoo prayer that ever existed.

My mother's face assumed the same darkness that had taken over Aparna's face before she ran out. It was identical. Then she opened her mouth to say something, stopped, walked closer to my bed, wiped my face with her saree, and said, 'You can't do that when there are other patients here, you could give them an infection.'

She knew it would make me angrier, and she seemed to revel in having said something so appropriate, so considerate, so classy in front of the other lady.

She turned and said, 'Sorry, Seema. He has a, umm, temper problem.'

I nearly screamed then, but I had resolved to die without ever saying a word to her again. Which I was possibly going to now. If you are fifteen, and admitted to a ward like this, and had surgery lined up, you could of course die. Then I remembered what I'd told Aparna, and I began to get really mad at myself. Why did I ask her to tell Nazia to see me after the surgery? What if I was dead by then? I was beginning to feel that lump in my throat again.

My mother might have seen the panic in my eyes, or Aparna might have sensed through that sibling connection of hers that I wanted to see her again, I don't know how, but a few minutes after my mother left the ward, my sister came back in to say bye.

'Can you tell Nazia to come see me before the surgery?'

'Are you going to die?' she asked.

She began to sob loudly. My mother peeked in and glared, and Aparna stopped crying immediately. The tears didn't stop, just the noise from her throat did. Her face crumpled like a newborn piglet, saliva dripping, her misaligned teeth on full display. It was at once gut-wrenching and sickening to watch.

'Don't cry here,' I said in that curt way my mother did, holding my index finger to my lips. 'And don't come to visit me here, you or your mother.'

I felt a bit relieved after they went away.

I looked across at Seema to see if she was judging me. She just shrugged, 'Hey, that never ends, by the way.'

'Hmm?'

'These fights with your parents. Somehow with age, it seems to get bigger, uglier, more painful.'

'Wait, do your parents hit you even now?'

She laughed, 'I meant pain here, and here,' she said pointing to her head and her gut.

'Here?' I asked, pointing to my throat.

'And here,' she said pointing to her butt, and we both laughed.

Seema's surgery went well. That gave me hope, maybe I too would live. She came to see me before she went home and said, 'Don't be so hard on yourself. And don't worry about what everyone will think of you now. They will see it the way you show it. If you show it to them for what it is, what you are, a brave boy, who went to hell and came back, they will also see it like that. Nazia will too, I promise.'

I couldn't say anything. I just lay there. That throat lump still very much there.

'Hey, you know, maybe your mum can write a comic book. She can call it "Burns Boy", you know, you can be like a superhero,' she winked.

'What's my superpower? Burning everything down?'

'You be the guy that can undo the burning. That's the kind of hero we both need now.'

Then she went away. I had little to do all day, and when my mother finally showed up, I forgot that I was supposed to be angry with her.

'Will you eat?' she asked, the way she did every day.

'No, I already ate,' I said, and only when she was patting my back did I realise that I had forgotten we were fighting.

'Your sister saw your friends at school,' she said. 'Some of them may be coming this evening to see you.'

I began to sit up.

'You want me to comb your hair, maybe help wash your face too?' she asked.

'Can I put on my own shirt?'

She nodded no. She helped me, quietly, without looking self-righteous, so I let her.

Neither Nazia nor Vinay showed up, even though I was dressed up, anticipating that handshake from Nazia the entire evening. I was feverish, I could feel the phantom of her hand on mine all day. By that night, I was ready to die. In the end, it was the happy couple's no-show that led to the outburst with my mother, the volcano of anger I had hidden under my silence for days.

'Are you finally happy I am going to die?'

'Nothing like that is going to happen to you, you hear me. Nothing.' She seemed to swallow a small sob. Seema wasn't around, so she could misbehave, and she would, I knew.

'You are crying now? Crying is indecent only when Aparna's doing it? Or is it because there's no one here for you to impress?'

'Where's all this spite coming from?'

'I am the villain, sure Ma!'

'I really don't have the energy for this.'

'You seem to have all the energy in the world when it comes to your writing, when you have to take care of your sick old relatives who come to stay with us. You don't have the energy to raise your kids? Is that it?'

'Nobody is as ungrateful as my kids. Just nobody,' she muttered.

'You really don't have to do anything. Just pray hard that I die while I get the surgery.'

She stormed out of the room in tears, but later claimed she'd waited in the corridor through the night. There was no way for me to know. Appa did not come to see me in the hospital. I did not ask about him. Aparna stayed away too. Only my mother kept on showing up. Making me angrier with her mere breathing.

'It's okay. I know you are in pain, and you can't take it out on anyone else. That's why you are mad at me,' she said the day before my surgery.

'No,' I shouted back. 'I am mad at you because you didn't care enough. You didn't come out soon enough. You weren't cautious enough. You ripped my bloody skin out and you made me need this bloody surgery. You wanted to hurt me. You always have.'

'Would I burn my own children alive? Would I really? You think?' She began to cry again.

'The day Aparna was born, I heard you tell Appa that you wanted me dead. Did you or did you not?'

All colour left her face. 'Words don't mean a damn thing,' she said.

'You are saying this, Ma? You are a writer. And it was not just me, you wished death on all three of us didn't you?'

She made swiftly towards the bed to slap me but then stopped.

'Get out, and if I die here, I want you to know you willed it. You and only you are responsible.'

With Seema gone, and my mother hiding from me in shame, I had nothing to do. Except wonder if I was going to spend the last day of my life alone in this pitiful state. I decided to look through the photo albums Aparna left with me on the day she brought mint. It was strange to see my old scarless self. I touched my hands and my neck in the photos. I wanted to become my own self again. I wanted to close my eyes and go back to being the boy in the photo. One that didn't need surgery, and would probably live beyond the age of fifteen. I flipped the page and found myself staring at my bare torso. It was a photograph of me drawing water from the well in our backyard, shirtless, in grey shorts. I missed the feeling of the water from the well just then. I could taste it in my mouth. They'd retained the well when they tore down an old bungalow to build our apartment block. The burning of my palms and fingers against the coir rope, the weight of the aluminium bucket as it came out filled with water from the well, the breath in my lungs, the tension in my legs and my waist . . . I could feel it all in my head, and then I wondered when I would be able to do it all next.

I wanted to strip, oil myself from head to toe, draw water from the well and pour that water over my body. I had done it, sulking, on a hundred Saturdays. Whenever I did it next, I would do it with joy. And fear. It made me sad and expectant. I wondered if this was how my mother felt when she had me. Looking at those photos made me sad. And hopeful. I thought of the photos from my future, and how they'd look. Would I always be scrambling to hide my arm, or would I let it be captured?

From pictures of me as a tiny baby in my mother's arms to pictures where I showed the beginnings of facial hair, I looked through all of them over and over. I picked some out of the album to peer closely at myself. I touched my neck from the past in the photo and began to feel a little better. I began to see myself live through this. Maybe even forget the pain, the surgery, and use the arm like nothing had ever happened.

How changed Aparna was from her surgery. You would never guess that she'd once lain in her hospital bed, unable to even pass urine on her own. She was back to riding my cycle without even holding the handlebar. She was back to running, skipping and playing badminton. All of it. But were we different? Is losing your appendix different from having to get your skin stitched up? Skin wasn't as deep actually, maybe I'd live? It was exasperating thinking about death. I decided to ask the doctor when I saw her next, instead of nodding silently at everything she said.

The night before my surgery, as I settled in to sleep, I found myself thinking not about my sister, my mother, Seema, Nazia, Vinay or Eliamma. But my father. Where was Appa? What was he thinking? He didn't even try to speak to me. Seema had calls, and the nurses always held the cordless phone to her ear even if she hadn't hurt her arms. Nobody called me. Why? Did my mother and he separate? Did she lie to me about him being in Iraq? I had seen pictures of him there. Appa had a civil engineering business and was recruited to build things in Iraq. He complained endlessly about the heat, but seemed to like the money he was beginning to see.

I could never figure out what she saw in him and why she was with him, my mother. He would show up all charming once every year, and she would throw herself into his service. She would also defend him for not showing up for me, as she'd always done.

You know he's got too many commitments.

He already does so much. So much.

I can take care of you. Can't I?

Where do you think money grows?

I knew he had to go abroad and work to support his 'lifestyle' and not his 'commitments', as my mother liked to call it. And yet no one dared challenge his authority. I said to myself the things I would tell him when I was older. I would set him right when I had my own money.

We lived comfortably enough, but weren't much better off than many of my friends whose fathers worked in regular Indian companies and went to work in buses. On top of it all, I saw my father once a year. Which made me wonder about what it is really like to be rich. If I didn't feel richer than someone, was I really rich? Was I even rich? How does one know if one is?

My father was a gentle, slow man. He liked to be thorough, and he planned his life impeccably well. For a while now, he had visited us only once a year, but in that time, he made sure to know everything there was to know about us. He was entirely devoted to us in that one month. He never once said no to us. He was always the one to tell us we could be or do whatever we wanted. The thing that really shocked me about him was how life seemed to work out for him. Even when everything around him was crumbling, he seemed to wear life light. As I sat there alone in the hospital, I also wondered if that was really the secret of his good life. The fact that he took care of things only and always from afar. He seemed to be doing well because he didn't really give a damn.

On the day I was discharged from the hospital, I still hadn't heard from my father. My mother showed up to take me home. We said our goodbyes to all the nurses and walked out. I was glad to be out, and to live after all. I wasn't feeling emotional the way Seema did when she left. I was happy. Like I could float high. I tried to not smile at my mother. And I tried to not let her burst my high, and ignored her even as she fed me inane, useless information.

'Looks like it's going to be really hot today.'

'This goddamn autorickshaw strike.'

'Better if we just head to the bus terminus and catch one from there. At least we'll get a seat that way.'

'I brought some water, but I am not sure it'll be enough. We'll have to stop somewhere for a cold drink, I guess.'

I'd have to be at home for a few more weeks and then I could go back to school. My mother was not even remotely partaking in this experience of revelling in the miracle that was my existence, that I had survived a ghastly ordeal. She was really just focused on the frivolous details of our commute. I had just got out of hospital. Alive. I could go back to school, live my life. When I asked Dr Annu if I could live a normal life, she'd said, 'Yes, of course. Just the exact same life as others. This does not interfere with your life, think of this as a short detour. You can go to school, college, work, get married, have children, grow old, all just the same as you were going to before the surgery. I can't guarantee you won't go bald though,' she winked and laughed.

What a great woman. I wished she were my mother just then.

'You'll heal faster if you're positive and upbeat, I promise,' she said. 'I realise you are having a difficult time with your family and the idea of the burns. If you want to, when you are comfortable, you can meet a psychologist and speak your mind. When you're ready. You can't see every scar.'

Remembering what the doctor said deflated me a bit. All the anger that I thought I had already spilled seemed to come back, an endless fountain of ill will had taken hold of my heart and head. By the time we reached the bus stop, it was incredibly hot. The air was hot, everything you touched was hot, I was sweating like I did when playing intense cricket in summer. Except now I was just walking in the shade, and very slowly at that. My mother was fanning herself with her saree, sweating too, carrying three bags in her hand, her forehead wrinkly, not at all stoic. Seeing her like that made me angrier.

When we reached the bus terminus, our bus wasn't there yet. My mother asked me to wait, and then I snapped, 'Where are you going?'

'Cool drink.' She sounded tired.

'I will go.' I wanted to get away from her.

'Where's this anger coming from anyway? I am doing everything, all of it, by myself. Can't you see?'

'You make me do whatever you want. You rip my skin out, you flirt with random men in our kitchen. You make me care for your guests, share my room with them, go with them to hospitals, listen to their sob stories, entertain them, run errands for them. And then they get better, go away and never come back to see me. No one even calls. And the rest just die. How do you think I felt in the hospital when no one came to visit? Not even my father?'

'It's my fault,' she said under her breath then.

'What?'

'I asked him not to come.'

'. . .'

'I thought it might be easier, you know, to raise money for your surgery there.'

'So you didn't tell anyone I am sick? In the hospital?'

I walked off to buy water without waiting for her reply. She tried to catch up, but was carrying too many bags, and kept tripping. I started to walk faster, holding my dressing in place. It was so hot I felt like I would burst into flames, and then not even a surgery would bring me back to life. The humid, hot air, my burning eyes, the fumes from vehicles on the road, it was all becoming unbearable. As I crossed an air-conditioned photo studio, I was tempted to go in and take in the cool air. I could get a photo clicked with all my bandages. I would make for a good first-aid poster model. Like the one we had hung in class as part of the fire drill with drawings of a boy wearing different kinds of bandages.

Names of bandages that would go on to become threats we used in class while playing cricket.

'I'll give you a Double Spica for Groin, wait, you asshole,' Vinay liked to shout.

Just then, a family of four, looking utterly lost, stopped me at the bus stop. I thought maybe they knew me. Then they explained.

'I have lost my wallet, and we are stuck here in Madras. I don't know anyone here. We need to go back home to Vellore. If you help me with any money you have, I will make sure I go home and send you a money order. I promise,' the father, dressed in a slightly muggy old white shirt and lungi, said. The son looked like me, and the daughter reminded me of Aparna. That hot day, just looking at them made me feel like crying.

'How will you go?' I asked.

'We just need the bus fare. The city is so dangerous, someone just stole all our money. So merciless,' the mother said.

I looked around. My mother was approaching. I was sure she'd want to impress me, that she'd want to be super helpful to this family. Upset that I didn't have any money, I began to walk away from them, saying, 'Amma is coming, you ask her. I don't have any money. Just enough to buy soft drinks. Sorry.'

Although I slowly walked away, I did linger to see how much my mother would give them. No less than a hundred rupees, I was sure. Then she'd smile smugly.

To my embarrassment, though, she treated the family like they were regular beggars, worse, like they were cheats. She brushed them aside and didn't even listen to them.

'I am too old to fall for this nonsense,' she said as she reached me.

Then I started to run, at first slowly, a jog, then fully run. I wanted to get away from her. Who was she? Who was this woman? I began to feel a little blinded by the sun as I ran. Then I noticed a cow coming straight towards me, and even though I was scared, I didn't step away from its path. I could hear my mother in the distance, shouting, 'Guru, don't run, you have just had a bloody surgery, come back.'

But I kept on running, sweat drops flying off me, the heat burning my skin and my face, my eyes too on fire. I was daring the cow to rip me with its horns. Just as I inched closer, it slowed down though, lifted its tail and began to pee. Then I began to pee too. Like the cow, I too relieved myself on the road. Not on the side, not by a tree or a transformer, not by a lamp post or behind a car. I unzipped my pants and peed on the road, like those disgusting men I saw on the roads from our classroom window and made fun of with Vinay and Nazia. Then the cow went on its path, uncaring.

'What the hell are you doing, go to the side, boy,' an old lady screamed as I looked around, zipping up. I wanted to see just how embarrassed my mother was. She had not seen any of it, she was still too far behind, and all the traffic between us had hidden what I had done.

I bought two colas and walked back to the bus stop. Still no sign of the bus. It was still hot, hot, hot, and there weren't too many people at the stop. I was beginning to feel faint, my headache worsened. Despite the drink, my throat was beginning to dry.

'I thought I could care for you myself. That's why I didn't tell anyone. If too many people know, they'd come and take over my time, and then I'd have to be worrying about cooking and cleaning after them. I wanted to be there for you, Guru. I am here for you now, aren't I?'

The Casio I couldn't yet wear showed two o'clock, 15 April 1999. The 5E finally appeared, bringing us both relief on that forty-two-degree afternoon.

'I am sorry,' she said as she climbed up the footboard of the bus.

Even though I could not stop asking myself questions about the bizarre events of that summer, I felt bad for her. I wanted to say to her, 'I guess you did what you could.' I may have. I can't remember.

2

And Now

Guru is sulking, again, and I'm growing tired of tiptoeing around the boy all day. It's been like this since we got home from the hospital. You know what the most confounding thing about mothering is? You think, I need to watch this child of mine, I see it in her eyes, trouble brewing like a cyclone in the Bay of Bengal; you think ah, yes, this other child of mine, this one's my safety net. All of it can flip, and suddenly you find you're in an upside-down universe. Apparently all it takes is one dreadful morning for whatever darkness is lurking under their tender skin to make its presence felt.

That's how you find out your sweet little angel has it in him to scream at you like he hates you. Your sin? Buying beetroot cutlets that he so loved once. *Do you even know me? Who eats beet cutlets?* He did. But then he forgot. For months he wolfed them down. You stood in long queues every day on your way from work to buy them for him. That's the only way you knew to be his mother. Labour.

He also hates it if you ask him, *are you hungry*, when he seems pointlessly dramatic. *Should I eat my tears too? People have emotions that are not related to food, Ma.* Such a knack he has for taking everything I say and turning it into an insult, a long-term wound. If you cannot bear the thought of someone hating you for some time, if not most times, I suggest not having kids at all.

His father is in his room, pretending to be busy. I also know that Sunil has begun to nap at odd hours just to avoid Guru. Come to think of it, apart from that time he chased me around town for 'friendship', and took everyone including his own self by surprise, it has been his nature to stay a bit aloof. (I was pregnant with Guru even before I married his father, that's how fiercely we chased each other.)

In the decades that followed we, Sunil and I have moved through the exertions of lust, the martyrdom of long distance, and somehow finally arrived at comfort and peace. He, bred in small towns, likes to say that we are two old trees rooted in the same jungle. Who's to say that this is not love? This silence of cohabitation. Breathing the same air without a quarrel, a kind of togetherness unmediated by noise. We have never made sense to others, certainly not to our kids. I am okay with that. Some things are like that.

If you ask me, a city bird all the way, I think of my marriage as a bus that's emptied halfway through on a long weekend when everyone in the city is off holidaying or has gone back home. It's just the driver and conductor making their way through empty roads till dusk, till they reach the last stop. The bus doesn't stop running just because it's empty, it does the thing it's meant to, and maybe the two even see a sunset along the way. No effort needed to converse. They're not at anyone's service, and so the air is light always. Even a bus that, at other times, to others can be a menace, can feel like home.

On Fridays we would go out. A matinee. Something with subtitles, because . . . old habits. (These subtitles though, they need to be bigger.) A movie and then a book a week gave us enough to chat about. Our digital paraphernalia, sundry acquaintances, home maintenance and the occasional chat with friends who dropped in for lunch or tea kept us busy the rest of the week.

But then, one day last month I bent down to soap my legs and felt a sharp stab: hernia. Now, Sunil and I will have to find a new rhythm. New ways fill our days that seem to be expanding and contracting, at once. Ageing is like that.

Guru and I though, we do not really talk to each other anymore. It's as if a wall has come up around us. I don't know who's in his life, for instance, or if he's ever happy, if he has a girlfriend, I suspect he's had a few over the years, but he has never told me anything about them, about how his work is going. All I know is that he interprets at conferences for car companies in Europe. How satisfying can that job really be, so far away from home?

Some months ago, I asked if he would translate a collection of my short stories from Tamil to French. I even offered to connect him with a writer and publishing assistant in Paris who could help. I thought he might like to meet a kind Tamil woman there. Prashanti and I met at a conference there, in Paris. Her family was originally from here. At first, Guru seemed interested, but then he stopped talking about it. Then I thought maybe he didn't like my stories, and that thought terrified me, even more than him not liking me anymore.

Chikkal. That's the word my mother's favourite astrologer used when he first drew Guru's horoscope. He made repeated calculations, counting the creases in his fingers. A knot, a complication, in Guru's future, who was barely a year old then. And then, to me, he said, 'You'll not see a daughter-in-law in your lifetime . . . you'll not, I don't see it anywhere.'

'He won't marry?' My mother sounded broken.

'Not in her lifetime,' he said, pointing to me.

It had not been a week since my discharge from the hospital. A surgery, however minor, at sixty-three, is more difficult than it sounds. Maybe because one ages swiftly when there's surgery involved. I could feel old age creeping up and becoming a habit, I had to snap out of it. When I was being wheeled in to the operation theatre, for a moment that conversation with the old astrologer flashed before my eyes, and I thought to myself, *On the bright side, he may finally find someone to marry if I don't make it out!*

I'd made it out, and somehow, I'd managed to avoid Guru all day. But I couldn't anymore because I had to ask him about the strange man in my living room I couldn't place. I made it to the kitchen slowly and whispered to Guru, 'I don't remember that guy who's asking for your father,' pointing to the sofa, 'do you? He even claims to have invested in something with your father years ago.'

'Amma, you don't, seriously?' The way Guru said 'you' made me wonder if I had done something to him, that man sitting on my couch.

I shrugged.

'Ma, vividly, I remember him vividly. He was here the whole day . . . oh, maybe you were away that day, now I get it, that's why.'

'That's a relief. So long as he isn't a crook,' I said.

In my other life, as an obedient government servant, I'd seen crooks of all shades. I knew of small ones, who forged big cheques for politicians, big ones that gave construction contracts to relatives and ate up public funds, bigger ones that bribed their way to acquiring fake bills running up to crores of rupees, teeny tiny ones that made up illnesses for the small change that came as medical aid or made bills disappear ahead of a probe for a tiny wad of cash, peons who moonlighted as loan sharks and lent to daily wagers.

But the first crooks I ever laid my eyes on, before I had set foot in the real world, were these two that had come to my home. I was never the same again.

I was twelve then. My grandparents had gone to Bombay by train. A couple of days after they left, an old man and his wife showed up at our door. My parents seemed clueless. I caught them asking each other with their eyes if the other knew who these people were.

We offered them water first to buy some time. Then we found out that these people knew everything there was to know: our names, what each of us did, what my grandparents were like, what each of us liked to eat. They even knew that my grandparents were in Bombay just then. So we couldn't stop at water. To make up for the embarrassment of not recognising them, we began to ply them with food.

The couple ate well, giving and withholding praise by turns, completely confusing my parents, who even opened up their bedroom out of guilt. The two napped for two solid hours there that afternoon and woke up to hot pakodas and coffee.

Before leaving, the man said to my father in this imperious, old-patriarch manner: 'As you know, we have been running an orphanage for two decades now.'

'Of course,' my father lied.

'What great service,' my mother added sugar to his lie.

'If you have important birthdays or anniversaries coming, we will be glad to serve meals for the fifty children in our hostel in your honour.'

I jumped to my feet squealing, *It's my birthday next month*, made to my piggy bank, broke it open and handed him everything inside. My mother glared at me, pinching the back of my upper arm very hard.

My poor father asked him, 'How much to sponsor lunch for her birthday? It is on the fifteenth of June.'

'Two hundred rupees, yes, that would be ideal,' the man said.

Stunned silence.

Then the sound of notes being counted.

Notes changing hands.

And then a quiet goodbye.

Two hundred rupees is nothing today, cheap change. Back then, it was half my father's salary. I got an earful from him for a couple of days, then we moved on. A month later, when my grandparents came back, we sat down to talk about that lunch. We cut each other off and corrected each other, my parents and I, narrating to them our version of the day, until we finally agreed on the events. I tried to draw them from memory. No use. My grandparents looked increasingly concerned. My grandmother even managed a nervous laugh.

'We have no such relatives,' she said, and then, almost to herself, 'Such nonsense.'

'Who in our family,' my grandfather asked, 'has the moral or financial authority to run a home for orphans?'

They were obviously wrong. We described the couple in detail. What they looked like: rotund, elderly, respectable, minimalist. What they wore: handloom. What they said: so much about us; so little about themselves. How they acted: authoritative, like elders did.

'But why did they do all this?' My grandmother was confused. 'For a meal and a nap? Are you sure they didn't steal any valuables?'

'No but . . . '

'What?'

'We donated two hundred rupees to their orphanage.'

' . . . '

'But they knew everything about us. It's impossible for someone to know that much. They even knew that you were on that train to Bombay!'

And then, my grandmother's face froze, like shocked women in illustrations that accompanied men's stories in Tamil magazines. Eyes wide, mouth an O. My grandfather looked at her, confused at first and then he too seemed to have heard thunder and seen blinding lightning. He slapped his forehead.

'It's our fault,' he said.

'We did this,' she agreed.

The couple had been in the same coupe as my grandparents on the train to Bombay. They befriended us, my grandparents said, *with humility and kindness*, learned everything about our family, even our home address, thanks to two days of eating and sleeping in that small space. They'd given my grandparents a whole other story: for those two days, they were pious Catholics on their way to their children's home in South Bombay.

That's how they knew to swindle us *that* well. They had studied my grandparents, dressed like them and acted just like them. They had scarred us all for good, and none of us ever again gave money to anyone after that.

Guru went out to get his father, came back and blurted out the words: 'I am not saying this to hurt your feelings,

Ma.' Whenever he said this, I knew that he intended to hurt me, and so I braced for whiplash.

'I remember this man clearly because it was that day. After Aparna was born, when you told us . . . you know? He spent the day at home that day with Dad, the day you went back to work.'

The boy was talking about that other day, one that had turned into an elephant taking up too much space in his heart. There wasn't much left for me.

The woman who said those words, the one who wanted them, my whole family, dead, that was a different me. From a different life. I remember her now like she was a friend, my younger self. I pity her, I do. When I say a different life, I mean a really different life, in which I was that obedient government servant, before I took a leave of absence and then never went back.

Guru was talking about a day I recounted to Aparna almost every other month. In the story I told her, of course, I eliminated what would be too much for her already fragile, even if wicked, heart. Maybe I so mythologised that day for her to hide from her what Guru had heard. Though I remembered every detail of that day, even the ones I did not acknowledge. Unlike faces, facts I had no problem remembering.

Ninety days after I had given birth to Aparna, I reported to work. My breasts wooden, stiff with milk. My body sore, still sensitive to every trifling disruption. My face glowing, projecting happiness that I felt nowhere in my bones.

Reluctantly, I woke up early and had a long, long bath, but it did little to make me feel whole again. My poor mother, who had disapproved of my every move for years, including having this child, was already up. Just like when I was a little girl, she was back to cooking for me. First breakfast, then lunch, then plenty of coffee.

I freely used her labour, and gave her nothing but sullen, moody outbursts in return. I felt, as daughters do at some point, that she deserved my contempt for bringing me into this world, deserved to slave away for me, just as I knew that this girl I had brought into being—thoughtlessly, selfishly—would think worse things about me. One day, she would definitely wish me dead, call me a slut, surely, tell me she hates me, and then when and if she had a child, she might find in her stone-cold heart some sympathy. It certainly wouldn't be worth it, I thought then.

By the time I got ready for work, Aparna was up and wailing, her pitch high, like some classical singer in training. I tried to swing her up and down in my arms, then in the saree cradle in my room, with nothing but the whirring fan for company in complete darkness. Then I tried to sing the only lullaby I'd ever known. *Vaave vaave vava vo*. No one in my family spoke Malayalam, but everyone sang this one lullaby in that sweet, alien tongue. She would have none of it though.

I hadn't named Aparna then. I was thinking of calling her something fancy, modern, but my mother wanted her to be named after her mother. In the end, Sunil named her. She had a pronounced chin, just like me and my mother, and my grandmother and my great grandmother. I remember tracing her chin when she was born, and wondering how many generations it went back, that chin. Did my hunter-gatherer ancestor-mother have it too?

I didn't know what my family tree looked like beyond my maternal great grandmother. Who knows, maybe my ancestors were kings, poets, thieves or maybe murderers. There was that apocryphal family story (which my grandmother insisted was a drunken oracle's lie) that one male ancestor of mine had forced himself on a woman who then cursed the clan. The idea of a rapist forefather did not seem too far-fetched to me. After all, I had myself pretended to have forgotten the advances of men and boys, my uncles and brothers.

My mother made me serve one of them, an older relative, a cup of tea when he visited us, and to this day I regret not spitting in it. He had lovingly caressed my cheeks when I gave him the cup, as if I was some daughter-figure and not the girl against whose thighs he had rubbed himself 'accidentally' coming and going when I was still pre-pubescent. When I told my mother once, choking on righteous anger, that events long suppressed from childhood had begun to erupt every now and then, shaving my nights thin, scooping up sleep as the price, hoping for awe, shock, love or at least faux sympathy, she barely blinked.

Oh, that's all?

I was livid. Was she treating this like it was cheap gossip that hadn't lived up to the hype?

You think you're the first woman to go through this. Others move on. You have to live life quietly.

Yes, from men in the family.

No, we can't confront them.

We must forget and move on.

I'll tell you what my mother told me—if we keep counting our relatives' sins, we'll not have any left. Must forgive, forget, that's what family does.

That's all I got from her.

That's when the idea that I, my mother, grandmother, foremothers, all of us, maybe going back to that ancient first woman, were molested by our kinsmen, the idea that the women who came before me too were serving these men, treating them like elders who deserved reverence, falling at their feet, asking for blessings at weddings and pregnancy announcement ceremonies, sometimes even putting up with hugs from men whose very scent could send them spiralling down to a dark place, made me hate, surprisingly, not these men, but my own body, my shrivelled-up, meagre self.

I even remembered the stench of that uncle's sweat distinctly. It came to me unbidden. Sometimes I imagined my own sweat smelled like his, and on those days, I washed my armpits over and over until I felt like I'd scraped the memory out. I let the hot water from the shower wash over me, but that hatred for my armpits never left me. It felt like the part of my being that was tainted by that stench forever. When I ran out of tears, I felt nothing but an icy coldness for the man in the depths of my heart. The images burned in my memory. I could summon them any time and carefully examine them with the expertise of a surgeon. I would wonder, was this the beginning, or that? Had I had allowed him to do things to me, given him permission? Sometimes I wondered if my eight-year-old self was somehow responsible for what I had endured. My mind had put me through torture like this for years, and some days it all seemed like my fault, some days it seemed like no one's, though always it felt like the burden was mine alone.

After feeding Aparna, I got ready to leave for work that day. I felt like a ghost that had left its heart back in a grave. My head still in a fog, my body refusing to move. Just as I opened the door to leave, the girl started to wail again. My slow descent to darkness began. Again.

Most mothers I've met, aunties, friends, colleagues, grandmas and cousins, admit to being traumatised by childbirth, or its aftermath; if it's not physical, it's mental, if it's not mental, it's social, if it's not social, it's the child's well-being; a pound of flesh motherhood wants, a pound of flesh it extracts. But we dare not talk about it. And our children, they can neither remember their own suffering from those months, nor ours. This is the former's curse, and the latter's blessing.

I wept for everything and nothing in those weeks. I prayed for Aparna to be easy, jujube, like Guru had been. With him, labour had wrung the life out of me—my doctor said it was the longest labour she had personally overseen. But Guru came out happy to be just staring at walls and the ceiling fan. Aparna was built differently, the girl was born with a personality so potent that it threatened to dissolve mine entirely. I hated that she would quiet down with others, with her grandmother especially, once even with the man who came to deliver the gas cylinder. With me, it was as if she remembered unresolved animosity from another life. Always agitated, body stiff as a brick, her face a ripe tomato, fists clenched and her tiny toe beans curled in. I walked up and down the house holding her to my breast as if something might go wrong if I didn't. If I had been anything of a friend to myself, I'd have told myself to use this gift; to sleep, to put my feet up, eat ice cream or watch something, go to a stupid movie or just stand by a window and stare. But I wasn't.

Some days I wanted to lose her somewhere, like at the fair that came up on Island Grounds, and then go back home for a few hours of deep sleep and precious silence. No sooner had that thought completed itself, I wanted to run outside to be run over by a bus. First, as punishment for having those thoughts, and then for the sweet release it might bring. A few moments of excruciating pain, and then deep, eternal sleep.

I kept waking up unprompted from sleep, as if I were being remote-controlled, to look at her, see if she were really breathing. It would then take me a good hour to fall back asleep, by which time she would wake up again. Some days (and nights of course) I wept for hours, thinking up sad little scenarios for her.

What if she dies?

What if she suffocates?

What if I drop her? Or shake her too fast.

What if she never gets her period?

Sometimes the what-ifs gently took over my sleep-deprived brain, and like parasites, reproduced there.

When poor Sunil or Guru or even my mother walked into the room, I spat mean, dark words at them. Those thought-parasites had licked each word, left their imprints on them. In those moments, I felt only hate. I didn't know where this hate came from. I knew that they were not lying when they said they cared for me, but all I felt then was a rage. Especially for Sunil, the very sight of him made me howl. Those days, I wouldn't have even cried if he'd dropped dead. And yet, it was only then that my mother began to treat him as she would a son-in-law. She'd been cocky when I had the son first, but now she thought I needed him, and my daughter needed him, more than he needed us. He could abandon us, and no one would care if we lived or died. So she changed herself; dressed well when he showed up, cooked for him, and even coyly teased him, bantered with him, to keep him coming. For my sake.

On the ninety-first day, my leave was up. I'd used all the earned leave; you got two-and-a-half days of leave for every month you worked. I'd been at this job for three years, working till the very day I went to deliver.

The retired government schoolteacher, Ganeshan, whose wife worked in the water department, caught hold of me that morning as I shuffled to the gate, cursing my sciatica.

'Why don't you quit?' he asked.

'Did you or your wife throw away your government jobs when you had your three daughters in the hope of finally having a son?' my mother snapped at him, muttering a good number of obscenities under her breath. I smiled as politely as I could and walked out. I wasn't in the mood to indulge her neighbourhood politics just then.

I hoped my forehead and its one thousand and eight worry lines wouldn't betray to the men at work the many demons I was playing host to. I sensed an increased hostility from them in the months leading up to my leave; were these men actually jealous of me? You'd think I was going away on a pleasure cruise, and not to give birth. My pregnancy seemed to provoke in many of them a very base emotion, even in the decent men.

As if summoning my strength, I wrapped the free end of my saree around my waist, the way I'd seen my Amma do it, and walked. But when I stepped forward, my thighs rubbed against each other, chafing, lighting up a new form of hatred for the world. I wanted to crawl back into the dark confines of the baby's room and sleep, with the devil gnawing away at me. I wanted to run back home and check in on my daughter. I wanted something to end. I did not know what. I was bad at this, so bad. At being a woman, a mother. I wanted to wallow in self-pity. To cry until I had cried all my tears, and to scream until I had wiped all of my bitterness from within. Still I walked.

On the way to the bus stop, I stopped at the temple. It shimmered with devotional fervour reserved for Fridays. All of the city had descended on the goddess to ask for unreasonable miracles. Slowly, I found comfort in the loud songs sung by women who were on the verge of turning into mediums for the goddess, their ululations gave me the strength I so craved. Everywhere, women in yellows and reds, their hair dripping wet, said silent and loud prayers. It was just the sort of distraction I needed. I began to feel better.

I bought salt crystals with whole black peppercorns in newspaper cones, offered it to the goddess and recited a few mantras. I was praying in front of the statues of the nine planets, when the priest, who'd recognised me, came up to me with flowers that until a while ago had been on the idol. I smiled brightly for the first time that morning, and dropped a coin on his plate. I pulled a bit of hair loose from my braid and wore the flowers.

Outside, the oracle I usually consulted sat on her makeshift crate bench. She was busy. A huge, unruly queue awaiting its future. I would come back in the evening.

I hadn't stepped out in weeks, hadn't spoken to the oracle in weeks either. Her words seemed to have a particular honesty, though I could no longer decide if I was simply following her predictions, like a map. Was I letting her birth my life's twists and turns? Or was she really a gifted clairvoyant? Whatever it was, she was capable of telling me about my future and that of my child's, of this I was convinced. When I was nineteen years old, she had predicted that I would have two children, both boys. And that I would take great care of my parents. She also later predicted my marriage with

Sunil. I wanted to ask her if I'd have one more child, another son. Would something happen to this new one? Was she going to die?

~

I was an assistant clerk, assigned a wooden bench to sit on for the entirety of my eight-hour shift. The bench had no cushion, not even the chairs in the office did, it was all rattan. And because only clerks were given chairs, I couldn't rest my back.

When I got to work, my super boss, the superintending engineer, a bald man with a luscious moustache, which is the only thing I can remember about him now, called me to his room. I remember holding the writing pad up to my breasts as I walked in. I did this whenever I went to see him. His eyes seemed fixated on that spot. Not just me, all the women in the office did this, and even that did not stop him. I was doubly careful this time.

He asked, 'Late on joining date? What is this, madam?'

'I was late, sir . . . ' I said, not meeting his eye, repeating his accusation but not giving him anything by way of explanation. What would I tell him anyway?

'I want Raju Sir's papers on my table by the end of the day, please leave only after I've signed off on it today.' He was curt, still staring at my large breasts that were hidden under my arm, under the pad, under the saree, under the blouse, under the bra.

Raju was my old boss. He'd retired when I was on leave. Corrupt as hell, he made his riches giving out contracts to men from political parties and their relatives.

I returned to my desk and found some man from Raju's family, a brother or cousin, who looked and smiled a bit like him, sitting across from me.

'Madam, Mr Rajamanickam sent me . . . about his pension,' he wriggled, shy, scratching his hair.

'He should get it next month.' I looked at my papers, and not at him. I knew why he had come.

'Thanks, madam.' The man slowly, deliberately, like an amateur stage actor, pulled out a brown-coloured envelope from inside his bag and pushed it gently towards me.

I was used to this.

'I will do my job. I get paid for it. You leave now, please.'

The man laughed loudly, embarrassed by my rebuff of his bribe.

'Thank you, madam. Thank you.' He walked away. No one else looked our way, but some of the other assistants sniggered.

When I had to use the restroom, I walked out of the office building, all the way down to the grocery shop, bought water packets and then went to the toilet. There was never any water in there. My colleague Nazreen madam's son was right to call that place a shit forest. Shit forest . . . shit forest . . . shit forest . . . he screeched the first time she brought him to office, his voice half adult, half child. It was the summer holidays, and her parents had refused to take the kid in. I wasn't sure if he called it shit forest because it was in an empty deserted part of town that had no restaurants, and our office was run-down and looked like a haunted bungalow, or if he had actually noticed the mounds of shit. People used the back of our office as an open toilet.

I got back to work, tallied accounts and readied papers for my boss to sign. He was meeting with someone.

'Madam, come, let's go for SKC,' one of the other assistants said then.

I wanted to wait, but my colleagues wouldn't listen.

'That baldie can wait, come, madam!' Nazreen madam, graceful as ever in her chiffon saree, her hair cut in a bob, laughed.

All five of us, assistant clerks, women from different departments, took turns paying for coffee and sweets each day of the work week at a canteen close by.

First, we ordered a sweet and shared it.

'Three by five right,' the waiter flirted with our table per usual, and brought three portions of rasmalai, split into five, in small white cups with saucers and spoons.

Then coffee. They gave away complementary savouries, usually Bombay mixture. In that intimate canteen, we caught up on life. It was the only thing I'd looked forward to when I set out from home that morning. Sweet kaaram coffee. Our SKC hour.

Nazreen madam's son, in class nine, had a girlfriend. She had been summoned to school by the principal and subjected to good old-fashioned public humiliation. *Does your son come to school to study or to act like a roadside Romeo?* The principal, a nun, looked too pious to be saying those words. Lakshmi madam's sister-in-law had come to stay with her, and had picked a fight over a new saree that Lakshmi madam's husband had given to madam. The sister-in-law really liked the saree and wanted to wear it to a family event. She had left their home crying when madam protested that she was yet to wear it. Some slapping ensued. Meenakshi madam's husband had another one of his episodes. This time, she had to physically restrain him from running out of the house screaming obscenities and hitting himself on the head. Keeravani, the youngest of us all, an eighteen-year-old, fresh out of school, a probationary office assistant clerk, had an inheritance war going on with her family. Her mother, who lived off her salary, had written a will leaving the poor kid out. She gave it all, the home, cash, gold, all of it to her son. He was married and had a home already.

'She hasn't left even a small bucket in my name, madam,' she said, eating her free mixture.

'You can't trust anyone in this world, dear. These are all lessons. Not your own mother. Not your children. Only your own hands and legs can you trust,' Nazreen madam said, and we all just nodded.

I had my share of new problems with the baby and the demons in my head, but didn't talk about them. They made me uncomfortable. So, I stuck to the usual ones. About Sunil's first wife and his two sons from that marriage with whom he spent four days a week. Thursdays, Fridays, Saturdays and Sundays were for them. They didn't even know of my existence; they thought he was out working when he left town three days a week. Didn't know that, in this other city, besides work, he had us, a whole other set-up.

~

I was his second 'wife', though legally, we weren't even married. I didn't avail of my paid maternity leave because the rule specifically said it was for 'married women'. I was too embarrassed to explain my situation to my boss, so I hadn't applied for maternity leave at all, even when he offered to clear it, whatever the complications. I did not want him to get the wrong idea about me.

Sunil was this small-time businessman then, Lakshmi madam's old neighbour. He was in the canteen having coffee one day and joined our table. Then 'ran' into me, he claimed, the next day at a clothes store near my house. He asked me to have coffee again. I knew he was married even when I'd just met him. He'd been upfront about it. And he always insisted that we were friends. Just friends. That's what he called us. *Just*. That was also the day he gave me a copy of Jayakanthan's *Unnai Pol Oruvan*, and changed who I was, taking me farther away from where my family and fate had intended me to be.

'You should read this. I loved it,' he said. For people who read, the idea that not everyone does is wild. I realised this when I told him that the last time I read a book, I was still in pigtails. Books were not a part of my life growing up. We had no time for leisure like that. If we did have free time, we spent it cleaning our shelves, dusting the loft, washing the containers in which we kept dal, rice and spice, washed our hair, or did chores for others in the family or in the neighbourhood.

'It's like walking down the road and peeking into someone's room,' he said to me about the book. He seemed to think I might like it more if it were sold to me like it was something of a scandal. In his defence, it worked. I ignored all the things that awaited my attention and read the book in one sitting in one single evening. I started reading it only so I could meet him again, and I knew that when I met him again, he would want to talk about the book. But when I began to read that book, from the very beginning, from the first line, I was confused but also at once in its thrall. A man could muster this much empathy for a woman? This very poor woman. Until then, I didn't know that books didn't have to be about pretentious things.

When I asked my colleague Chidambaram, whom I had found annoying because he was perennially lost in books instead of clearing pay bills in time, where he got his books from, he suggested I enrol in the Egmore library. This is how I came to read everything Jayakanthan ever wrote. Then I began to read. Really read. Man, woman, small, big, novel, magazine, I'd read anything that held words and the worlds they held. Then Chidambaram told me one day that one of those writers that I had been reading in a little magazine worked in my department, and was using his wife's name as a pseudonym. I was both ecstatic and jealous. Many of the writers I admired, it turned out, were government servants, so I figured that maybe someday I too could write. Through those weeks and months, I couldn't wait to discuss what I read with Sunil. I quickly surpassed him, because I had always been tenacious.

I didn't ask my oracle about Sunil then. What was I to ask that celibate woman about my feverish desires for a new man who had me eating out of his palm? He wasn't extraordinarily handsome, that's not why it all turned out this way, but he had the eyes of a lost man looking for something. And at long last he had figured out that I was what he was looking for.

He dressed in crisp half-sleeved shirts and trousers that fit well, his full head of straight hair was neatly combed back. He had a well-kept moustache, and a little pockmark on his forehead only made him more handsome. He looked better than me in every respect. His skin even glowed, that well-off person glow. He seemed better off than me too. He seemed educated; I was just a high-school pass. And yet, he saw something in me, and that made me sympathetic to his every move.

When he wanted to meet me, he'd look at me like he were begging me for my time, as if I could, would, should turn him down. He would ask in English, 'Shall we go get SKC?'

I found myself nodding eagerly every time he suggested we drink coffee. I learned everything about him. In hindsight, what man wouldn't love to build himself up with some young woman listening to him in awe?

'I am an atheist, actually, which is a big problem for everyone except me. My wife is just very devout.' When he said that they were beginning to drift apart over the question of faith, and that she wanted him to pray, I announced to him right away that I prayed. That it gave me hope and gave me a discipline and routine that I liked. It gave me things to do that were not work. It made me relate to other humans who too had the humility of character to surrender, who were not full of themselves, who recognised the smallness of their presence in this vast world. It told me to wake up early on Fridays and walk alone to the temple. I could ask for things in prayer that I could not ask of any person. I liked that. *I like asking for the impossible.*

When I said those last words, I knew I had said too much. Because he looked smug. As if I was telling him that I was praying for him. But he didn't say anything. In reality, I was only interested in his interest in me. I was not looking to replace his wife or become a vampish stepmother figure to his children at all. I never even met them until my own children were old enough to understand they had half-siblings.

'I started reading as a young boy during the physical activity period in school because I was asthmatic.'

'I just like to sneak in sweets before bed. But then, as soon as I eat a piece of sweet these days, I want something spicy, and it always ends up reminding me of you, of our SKC. Sometimes you show up in my dreams.'

I enjoyed listening to him embarrass himself like that, but months passed in this manner. He came to meet me every day he was in town, making up some excuse or the other, but was always calm, there was never a misstep.

When I figured out that he was all talk, I began to withdraw. It didn't seem to me like he was going to end his marriage. What was the point? I went my way and got engaged to someone else, someone my mother picked. The minute he heard of my engagement though, he hovered around me again, with eyes that begged for something more, but lips that spoke of friendship. An honest companionship that he would hate to lose, he said. It was new to me. In the kind of lower-middle-class homes that I knew, women did not have male friends. If a man was so much as sighted around a woman, she began to gain a bad reputation, and then she was quickly married and sent away. Always to someone else.

I don't know how to describe this irrational idea I had in my head then—although I was to marry a different man, I felt that somehow, somewhere, maybe in the future, maybe in a different world, Sunil and I were already lovers. Here, in this universe, at that time, we were simply waltzing in and out of each other's life, taking the other for granted, but surely, we were fated to be united, I thought, at least once in this lifetime.

We never transgressed in those early days. I didn't cheat on my fiancé, nor Sunil on his wife. I found ways to stall my impending wedding, yes, I was always reading too much into Sunil's gestures, yes. But cheat? No. Whenever we met, which was often, and in the presence of my betrothed, there was that confusing electricity of eyes held in place for a few seconds, when all the world around us, Sunil and me, blurred into oblivion.

I used to think love was not merely physical. Love could just be a constant in your life, you could meet them often, and that would suffice. At first, I drew some comfort from that thought, but then I quickly realised that I was always dissatisfied. I often went home furious after meeting him. The man I was with, Dileep, seemed oblivious to this, or he pretended to not notice the fire in our eyes, even though he sat right there with us every other day. I think he was terrified of what that fire might engulf and chose to ignore it.

After a year or so of dodging my own heart, I felt like things were too comfortable for Sunil. He showed no signs of agitation ever. Even when I was with this other man, he was always calm. I decided to complicate things, I decided not to play so nice, I decided he needed to demonstrate he cared for me. I decided to transgress just a tiny bit. I would do nothing provocative, not even a thing vaguely indicative of sex. All I would do was throw a tiny little pebble in the perfectly calm waters to see if the dangerous, exciting thing that lurked just under the surface rises to the top. I wanted to see him come undone, even if just a little. Neither of us would do anything, I thought. I just wanted to see if he ever felt as helpless as I did.

I asked Sunil to watch a movie with me on a day my fiancé was out of town. He was confused at first, searching for answers. I gave nothing away. Sunil, who until then thought I was the epitome of what was appropriate, prudish, didn't know what to make of me. He agreed, but I read something close to worry in his eyes. I asked him to pick the film. He chose a French film, a free screening at the Alliance Française. I thought it was to avoid being seen with me in a regular theatre, but my friends thought it was so he could watch kissing scenes with me. I didn't care either way.

That day, at the first movie I saw with him, which was about a woman who finds both a handsome man and that elusive last ray of the sunset, I controlled myself admirably in the dark of the projection hall. I managed to hide my needs—to hold hands, to touch his face, rest my chest against his. When the movie ended, reassured by my own strange calm, I walked out of the hall. Then it happened, he quickly unravelled. Just as we walked out of the theatre, he slipped his hands, cold and sweaty, into mine, sat me on his scooter and rode us to his room. When we reached the deserted stairway of the building, we kissed. Our every touch fire, a burning, an intense explosion. We undressed in the dingy room, he with consummate ease, I clumsily, though he didn't seem to care or notice. I thought then that I would burst into a million shards of joy, smug, even evil, joy. We met every day he was in town, for weeks, months. I felt so glorious that the arrogance of my happiness engulfed me entirely. My mother's biting disapproval, her beatings and threats to stab me while I slept, or to immolate herself, most certainly did nothing to dissuade me. Not even my fiancé's entire clan showing up and threatening to finish me off could stop me. Whore, whore, whore, whore. By now, I was used to that chorus wherever I went. No one else had what I had, I thought, if they did, they would understand. We felt love, its violent tremors coursing through our beings.

When my stomach started to show, he introduced himself as my husband to my friends. I did my best to ignore the look of disgust in the eyes of his acquaintances.

I expected to be ostracised of course. Instead, amusingly, to many men, especially older male cousins, I instantly became an object of pity, and to several women in the family, a thrilling secret friend. They were, obviously, outnumbered by those who wanted nothing to do with me, but then, even this latter lot kept in touch with the men and women who were talking to me, if only to get their dose of scandal. Those who came to see me ensured I heard all the things said about my mother and me. It was always only about the two of us, for some reason.

What could the poor girl do? Her mother was milking her dry, living off her.

If it were my daughter, I would have murdered her and gone straight to jail, my head high.

Is he enjoying the company of both mother and daughter?

If all this is happening under the mother's nose, imagine how faithful her mother must have been?

It was exhausting, and yet soon this became my new life. Many wanted me to know, in private, that they were okay with me even if they never did invite me over. They sent word with their children; they dropped in for a surprise coffee sometimes. I was both grateful and suspicious. I had no time to have an opinion on it.

I didn't allow myself to think about anything. Thinking involved stopping, and I was scared to stop. If I stopped, I was worried it would all be over, and so, in those days, I did not know what I was doing, even though I was the reckless orchestrator of all that had come to define my life and family.

I did not allow anything or anyone to take from me this happiness and power, the strength and pleasure I was experiencing. Then I gave birth to Guru. In the early hours of a warm day, a 3.1 kg baby boy.

~

There were unspoken rules about what we could discuss in that hour my work compatriots and I spent drinking coffee. None of us mentioned the good in our lives for fear of the evil eye. Occasionally, we showed off a new gold trinket, but no more. We never complained about anyone in the office either. Experience had taught us that gossip at work was like wildfire, there was no way to control it, it only spread, grew larger and destroyed more and more.

We spent an hour on this and that and returned to our tables. I liked to clean my desk before leaving. So, I set about tearing old documents that I did not need, it was a calming ritual, and then filing away new papers in the right files. When I finally I prepared to leave for home, that all-too-familiar feeling came crawling back, working its way through my skin.

I waited for my boss, though the old creep had left word with the senior clerk that I could leave. I waited till late in the evening, alone in the office hall, revelling in the quiet. Reading a cinema gossip magazine the clerk had lent me. When the officer finally arrived at eight, slightly tipsy, he was surprised to see me there.

'I asked you to leave.'

'Sir, these are sensitive papers. I did not want to leave them on the desk.'

He signed. 'It's good to have you back, madam,' he said, eyes still on my breasts.

I skipped two buses that were full. I waited to see if a point-to-point or a ladies' special 5T bus would show up, but no such luck. I caught the third bus that came, it seemed just as full if not more. There were no empty seats. I stood, holding on to the steel bar next to the conductor. I was no longer pregnant, so no one offered me a kind look or a seat. Instead, I was just that plump-from-childbirth woman who deserved to be mauled by lechers. Or crushed by bodies that hated how much space mine took up. I swore and promised to myself that I would lose weight to become my teen reed-thin self again. Every time the driver hit the brake, a pain seemed to emanate from my bones, then passed.

It was all okay. I was glad to be distracted, even if by my hatred for these bus beings. I stopped in front of the temple for a minute. The oracle had gone home for the day. From gods and their mediums, I needed guidance on days like this. My soul felt parched.

I walked back home as slowly as I physically could. And just as I crossed the threshold, a mad scramble began around me.

Sunil.

Guru.

My mother.

The baby.

I felt like the human leeches all wanted my blood.

'Why don't you all just die. Or kill me. Especially this one,' I said, pointing to the wailing child. I wanted Sunil dead, and for Aparna to kill me. But of course, Guru would infer the worst meaning from everything I said.

That was my last day at work. I picked up a card the next morning from the post office, wrote to the chief engineer, asking for leave 'due to personal circumstances', and then sat on a No. 11 bus that went up and down half the city, doing nothing at all. T Nagar to Broadway. Broadway to T Nagar. I didn't send in a resignation letter, just that leave letter, in case I needed to go back to work. Sunil could abandon me, just as my mother predicted, go bankrupt or die. If I went back and put up with a few denied promotions, I would have a job, even a pension until I died. Too rational for a woman who threw away a life of decency, who birthed children out of wedlock and stopped going to a respectable job for no reason. My mother was heartbroken by my decision. But I know why I quit. I wanted to force Sunil's hand, wanted him to surrender, and in order for him to surrender to me, I had to annihilate myself. And then I was gradually reborn, as the years rolled by and the children grew up.

My mother hung around long enough to raise my children, although she never forgave me for throwing away the security of a government job. When I had a handle on them and my own self, she went.

Then, something steely, something akin to my mother's resolve came alive in me. After she passed away, I was so confused that I became my mother. It was slow, and I found great comfort in finding myself in my mother's image. I swapped my cotton sarees for Vareli sarees, wash and wear she called it, and loved how low maintenance it was. I let my hair grey but never let it down or open, I always tied it up. But for me, the real challenge was cultivating acceptance, a stillness that seemed impenetrable to outsiders. Agitation was always meant for my mother herself or the person who caused it. No one else needed to be involved. She never made a scene in front of others. In private, she even threatened to murder me, but in front of others, she always stood by me. That was my mother. She was no saint. But absence certainly made her seem so.

After my mother died, I spent a large part of my life taking her place as the caregiver for the old in our family in the house that she had left for me. Guru disapproved of it in his own quiet manner. He never had any space. But I needed to have others around. To make up for my missing husband. To act as a buffer between me and my children. When even other people were no longer enough, I found refuge in words.

Then Aparna was born. Sunil left his wife for good. I never asked him to, he just did. Slowly, my mood improved. We registered our wedding, two children in tow. I began to feel both powerful and resentful. Living together all days of the week seemed unnecessary after years of time away. And so, like a fool, I agreed to living apart again. I didn't care then because my mother was still alive. He found building work in Iraq when his business began to stagnate here.

But then my mother died.

~

Perhaps Guru brought that day up innocently, but then again, who knows how many years children wait patiently to extract revenge on their errant parents? So maybe he meant to hurt me.

He was not inside my head, so how would he know what my life was like in those days? Like the fact that Dileep, the fiancé I had abandoned to jump into bed with Sunil, was the reason his accident took a turn for the worse. I was mad with guilt about it, I thought Guru would die because I was a bad woman.

On the morning of his accident, I let both Guru and Aparna loose because I needed time for myself. When they were children, I only allowed them pleasures when I could get some myself. My parenting style was a bouquet of these sorts of pettiness. Things between Sunil and me had come to a standstill, windless as middays in Madras. We barely spoke to each other when it wasn't about finances. That's the price I paid for forcing his hand, for tying my finances to his fortunes. The cheques for school fees, the groceries, the medical bills, the loan sharks and the EMIs, those were our concerns. This is exactly what Sunil had sought to escape in our early years together.

He must have done all this with the other wife. In those days, I took care of my finances handsomely, by my own self, with my government salary.

Before I married him, before I sculpted the man he is today out of his old shell, I saw him three days a week. Once we married, I saw him only once a year. I kept waking up to nightmares of his encounters with other women wherever he travelled. Of his many other families. Of having to meet his first wife some day in private and being spat upon by her. I was depressed, and in the midst of this loneliness and imagined cruelty, I tracked Dileep down. I wrote to him, asking for some time to speak to him. He didn't respond. I kept writing. Until one day he called me to ask me to stop writing. I asked him to come see me. That seemed to work.

We only met outside, and only on the days Guru feigned an extra class and went out to some bakery with his classmates. I dragged Aparna along and met Dileep for dhoklas. We always sat by the door, on bar stools, facing the road. Me, Dileep, and in between us, Aparna, whose eyes said 'whore', like the eyes of the men at work when I was pregnant. I ignored her, and allowed the new tension I felt with a man I had pushed away feed me back to life.

On the morning of his fire accident, I told Guru we were having a special visitor, and that he must be gentle with this man.

'He stammers so you cannot make fun of him or laugh or imitate him, okay?'

'I am fifteen,' he shrugged.

Aparna knew of course, and had made so much fun of him that she had begun to stammer a little herself sometimes, involuntarily. I had to shake her down to stop.

I didn't tell her he was coming.

I invited Dileep over to lunch, not to fulfil some weird fantasy, but to show him my world. To apologise for what I had done to him, because I felt that might make me stop fretting about Sunil doing to me what I had done to Dileep. I also wanted to show him a story that had just been published in a women's magazine. I had named the hero Dileep. A spirit helped Dileep change his destiny in the story's universe. He got the girl he was meant to be with, a modern bombshell. The Dileep of that universe also got to gloriously cast aside a snooty girl with roving eyes his family wanted him to settle down with.

The magazine's illustrator had given Dileep bootcut pants, an animal print shirt and a sharp, sexy moustache. He had one leg on the floor, and the other on a boulder. A cigarette in hand. On his shirt, where his pockets would have been, on either side, were photos of two girls. On his shoulder, a fairy-like faint figure. I had titled the story 'Three Devis'. It was at once an apology and an attempt at righting my wrong.

Back in those years, whenever any little thing went wrong in life, if I missed a bus, if I received a bad review, if a relative staying with us passed away of illness, I couldn't stop thinking that it was punishment for that other thing I did. Life had knocked all cockiness out of me. In those fragile years, when I waited for something to go very wrong, things in fact went well for me. Except for the mistrust that briefly crept between us, my husband and I held on. He didn't cheat, at least he ensured I never found out. I didn't cheat.

In all aspects of life, including writing, the more I waited for something bad to happen, the better it seemed to get. Instead of celebrating though, I got more anxious.

On the morning of the fire accident, Dileep and I were in my kitchen. I was sitting on the countertop, he was standing next to me. Both of us were drinking coffee even though the day was a furnace. I had just begun to show him my penance, my story, when Aparna rushed into the kitchen and climbed on top of the countertop next to me. Dileep moved away from me as soon as she entered the kitchen, and then I spotted a smug, cruel smile on the girl's face.

What a menace that child was then. She spent the entirety of her childhood practicing being a world-class brat. Then she became an adult, and it was as if someone had turned off the mischief-maker switch. She was suddenly an upright, stable, honest, reliable horse of a girl. Better than me in every way. If she were to find out about my twenties, she, I've no doubt, would be shocked. But even now there's a voice deep inside me that always says, 'Watch out with this one. Never know what she can pull.' That's the kind of rascal she was.

then

I was called to her kindergarten school and given a nasty dressing down by her teacher because she was found suckling on a boy under the desk. From there on, it only got worse somehow, until she went to college, when she quietly transformed. The unruly, unpredictable child sent her soul back up and swapped it for a sparkling new soul. I suspect my mother might have said the same about me if she'd seen me after she died.

On that day, Aparna, Dileep and I made awkward conversation in the kitchen for a while, and then I lost patience.

'Go to your room,' I said under my breath.

'Why?' She was defiant.

I got off the countertop, pulled her down too and sent her out. My daughter was behaving like my mother might have done. If I wanted a man, I could have him without a living soul ever finding out. Aparna was too young to realise this, and reluctantly went out. A second later, even before I could turn around, she slammed the kitchen door on my face. I didn't lock it. I remember because she opened the door again two minutes later. When she entered the kitchen this time, Dileep was saying goodbye to me. He came closer to me, wanting to say something, but just at that moment we both burst into laughter.

'Look at us.'

It felt good to hear him laugh, to have him breathe so close to me.

He said, 'Thank you for the story. I am going to frame this. How handsome you made me look.'

I straightened up, held him by his shoulders, and said, 'I owed you this.' I needed it more than he did. We said goodbye, awkwardly holding each other's shoulders. In that moment, Aparna forced the door open, wagged her finger at us. Her little eyes screaming 'I knew it!' We were standing a feet apart, only holding each other's shoulders with both our hands.

She slammed the door again.

'Kids are stupid,' I tried to explain to Dileep, wiping the fluster off my skin.

'It won't be trouble?'

I shrugged to show him I didn't care. Relieved to be rid of my daughter, I climbed back on to the countertop.

'Would you like another coffee?' he asked.

I thought he was going to leave, but Aparna's accusation had only made us both defiant.

'No one's made one for me since my mother died.'

He then made me a cup of coffee. It was the most I had been seduced in years, and I felt like I owed Dileep that much, that afternoon.

Guru tiptoed in and ran out with something. I didn't notice what he took. He closed the door behind him, the respectful boy. He knew even then that privacy was important. I offered it to him every now and then in exchange for some for me.

It might have been a perfect day. A beautiful afternoon, if not for what happened next.

First the sound. A noise so loud that it exploded inside me in a fear and fury I haven't felt since.

Dileep and I both made for the kitchen door, but it was jammed, just wouldn't budge. He had the presence of mind to slam the door with the crowbar in the kitchen rather than attempting some stupid macho thing like slamming into the door with his body.

I saw Aparna right in front of the door, in a state of shock. I turned around and saw my son ablaze. This is the only explanation I have for what I did next—I felt then that the right thing to do was to get that shirt off him before the fire engulfed him further. It threatened to do so. Then I dragged him to the backyard and poured cold water on him from the well until I was sure he was safe.

I could still pick up this stick of a boy. I ran to the bus stop, got in an autorickshaw and made the driver go so fast the three-wheeler nearly tipped over as it turned a corner.

Just as I began to weep, began to think somehow that this was my fault, it was all of course because of my bad character, the foulness of my soul, Guru, with his voice hoarse said, 'I am going to die, just as you wished.'

I didn't say a thing to him then because I couldn't stop, had to keep moving, walking, running. I ran even faster when we finally reached the hospital. After I settled him in the ward, I remembered home. All the peace and seduction of the afternoon had been emptied out of me. It was in that moment that an irrational idea took its place. And has never left me since.

The thought of Dileep and Aparna alone made my stomach churn. What might he reveal to her? What would she ask him? What could he do to get back at me—for how could a mere story in some two-bit magazine make up for what I had done?

Did he cause this accident somehow maybe?

I had found a way to make it not my fault and my fault all at once. It was the perfect disaster, and I had cooked it myself.

It was time for me to call Aparna.

3

Still Here

'Spritzing for thirty-one days straight this month,' I texted Amma.

Everything in this house is mouldy and smells like a lunchbox that someone forgot to clean. The kids' clothes, our furniture, the walls, even the ceiling. I think I last saw the sun seven lifetimes ago. It's the last day of August, and I can't remember the last time it wasn't drizzling. On and off, on and off, like a geriatric dog attempting to pee. Monsoon in the western ghats, I was told, was a romantic, sensuous thing, but all it means is that your underwear won't dry at all. It made me want to scream into a pillow.

But I put up with it instead of going home to wonderfully dry Chennai this past month, that's how much I dreaded the prospect of spending time with the family.

Flights *have* been taking off from Mangalore all through this sloppy wet month, and I think I have finally run out of excuses. I've in fact been lying about work and hiding out here in Manipal, but Guru has had his yearly dose of mother superior. He wants out.

I've been working from home for a year now and could have gone over to help Amma recover from her surgery, but I froze for some reason when she called. Guru is rushing off to Paris before I reach home, tgfsm (a useful acronym I have my son to thank for, thank god for small mercies). The thought of Guru and my mother in a hospital had sent me rushing back to the comfort of Restyl all over again. My psychiatrist, who's this young thing that works at the medical college here, asked me to 'just roll up a joint and go chill'. She even offered to source some for me.

I scowled: herbal supplements, grounding exercises, mindfulness, lavender essential oil and barefoot walks on overgrown grass were for beginners.

My mother called to tell me about her surgery but then spent forever going over the details of *my* time in the hospital, when I had to have that stupid little surgery. We did have a good laugh at my dear departed grandmother's expense. Paati was absolutely convinced I got sick from riding a boys' cycle—Guru's stunning green Streetcat—all day long.

Guru had tried to teach me how to ride that cycle, but I headbutted a tree on the very first day. I mean, how could I turn the handlebar to the right when I didn't know what a handlebar was? He spat a few instructions, left me with the cycle and ran off. The next morning, Guru was still grumpy, and Amma, who didn't know how to ride a bike herself, was no help. I decided to take the plunge myself, how hard could it be? (Very, apparently.) I was so short that I had to sit on the crossbar, a feature only in boys' cycles. I badly wanted a shiny pink Ladybird, with a basket for flowers, but my parents just couldn't wrap their head around the idea that their two children needed two cycles. So, I learned to ride sitting on the damn crossbar. It was supremely uncomfortable, like someone kicking my lady parts whenever I braked. But I was a girl possessed.

Then one day it just vanished, mother promise. I was at my Maths tuition teacher's home, and had locked the cycle. I think I did. Poor Guru, I still feel bad for him. It's true I liked to hide people's keys and scratch them out of family photo albums when I felt hostile towards them. But it was pretty stupid of Amma to think I 'lost' the cycle out of spite.

'If you keep this up, we are going to have to send you away to a hostel or something,' she roared.

'It's not so easy to lose something this big. God will show you what happened after you die, and you'll see some thief stole it! You big stupid Ma.'

To be fair, Amma wasn't overreacting. I was a full-on busybody at nine. Earlier that year, when Amma ran off to the hills to write, leaving Guru and me with Paati, an epic drama unfolded back home. Amma had been awarded free stay at some prehistoric bungalow in Coonoor where she planned to finish her novel, and was kicked about it, but fate (and I) had other plans.

Until I was finally diagnosed, my grandmother thought I was 'just doing drama' over some stomach pain. She figured I couldn't stand the thought of Amma having even a teeny bit of time to herself. My grandmother even forced me to go to school when I was shaking from pain and holding my stomach. Even when I vomited the dosa and seemingly radioactive green chutney she force-fed me, I had to go to school. For a whole week, she made me drink buttermilk with bitter fenugreek seeds because, according to her, 'there was no bigger cure for a stomach ache'. First-class liar, that woman. Then finally, when I wouldn't just drop the act, however much she threatened to kill me, she grudgingly took me to Child Trust Hospital. Another week of tests followed while I was nearly dying of pain: ultrasound, blood, urine, stool. And then came the barium test and the grand reveal. What a humiliating couple of weeks. Good times. I've always wondered whether Amma might have taken me more seriously than her mother did. I pitied Amma for the first time then, for the kind of childhood she must have had with that strict officer for a mother. She had rushed back from Coonoor and cried her eyes out.

This too she spoke about in full detail when she called about her hernia. After my surgery, I was wheeled out wearing nothing but that gaudy blue gown, still heavy with sedation. I tried to complain to her about the operation theatre being cold as Antarctica, but everything I said came out as word khichdi.

'When you woke up, the first thing you asked for was your brother, you didn't even bother with me, you wanted just him,' Amma said. Of this, I had zero memory.

When I'd read Amma's novel as a kid I could see the hills, the happiness, total shanti and nirvana she'd found, without us, while I lay twisting in pain. I recognised it all from the photos she kept hidden in the locker of her steel almirah; I'd snoop around there to look for money.

'I am still so thankful for those few weeks in the hills. Otherwise, I might have never started off that first novel, you know,' she said.

'I know, Ma, you'd have just dragged your feet, stuck in this ocean of samsara,' I teased. 'This was your book about a Gandhian playwright.'

'You remember!' When I asked her about her work, instead of pretending to know nothing about it, it made her happy-happy.

Of course I knew all about it, the novel she started while she hid from her bastard children—though Appa always liked to call us his children of love. Her book was based on the life of a real but not-so-famous woman writer of detective fiction who lived in the 1920s Madras. She borrowed generously from her own life too.

I knew all this because I was bloody good at digging through my parents' and my brother's stuff when they weren't around. It's why I keep a tight leash on my youngest who really likes to snoop too.

When Amma's novel was published, it did a number on me. I'd already seen her notes on the hotel's stationery and on random shreds of paper in her luggage way before she finished that novel. She had scribbled as if in a rush in that horrible handwriting of hers. I found bits like this everywhere in her room, which had barely any furniture, but piles and piles of books on the floor, all along the walls. That's how I knew she meant every word she said in her posh book.

Wood Garden Country Club
Coonoor

Under my balcony was a cluster of lilies, all green, except for one with three pink flames in the middle. Moss covered every conceivable surface. Two slender pines stood next to each other gracefully, greens of every hue, and flowers I had never seen before in brilliant reds and purples on trees everywhere. Some trees were dry, for it was still autumn, others green, light and dark, and in between were patches of the mountain terraced for cultivation. They'd soon bear English vegetables and fruits.

The clouds came in each morning at the same time, they assembled at ten, and then soon it began to pour, I watched it all in leisure with a cup of orange pekoe I brewed myself. Mist drifted through mountaintops like smoke from a beloved's kitchen, like someone sending me an invitation to dinner.

Sharp, pointy rain pattered like little stones on the roof, competing relentlessly with the birds and the many-hued insects. The birds and insects always won. Eventually, come dusk, the rain went quiet. In the evenings, the birds were even more restless.

Though the grass and the trees stretched out like endless carpets, cool and inviting, the ground was infested with leeches, and if you weren't careful, you'd go to your quarters with big fat bloodsuckers attached to your feet, itchy and painful. Monkeys broke the roof tiles more often than the weather did. They'd made a game of breaking the tiles and swinging swiftly from the roof to the floor and back up, both to amuse themselves and scare people off.

As the cold came like a thick blanket in the evenings, a merciful fire crackled and came alive in the main room.

It was always cold, even through the day, and so one had to remember to keep things warm. A small fire in the fireplace in your room, boil water half an hour before your ablutions, suchlike. The mountains taught you to lean on yourself, to care for yourself.

By evening, my hands went numb with the cold. It was to tackle this that I began to write swiftly. I also needed to keep up with my thoughts, and also feel my arms ache, alive, fertile, because things were too still in front of me, always the same. Comfortingly the same. It felt like I was in a duel to see who would win. The wind always did—my hands froze even though my mind still raced with words. Then I'd run into my room, where the fire worked to keep everything warm, and wrote until sleep came.

Dinner was always a generous spread, hot and fresh. Here, I finally learned what they mean when they say you can taste the earth and the rains; the best I'd eaten in a long, long time. The best I'd felt in a long, long time. The most content I'd been since I met the man in my life.

To be in my own presence.

To reclaim my own mind and body.

To be my own self.

Not a wife, not a concubine, not a mother, not a daughter.

Me, a writer.

~

What was an idiot kid to do with evidence of her mother feeling tip-top having got rid of her kids? I am happy for her now of course, not back then when I was a true-blue drama rani. When my folks' happiness didn't involve me, it felt like it came at my expense. With my dad gone all the time, I felt senselessly homesick if Amma wasn't around. I didn't have the vocabulary for it then, but now I know that it was just longing.

The idea of Amma going on a vacation without me was also shameful to me, and like all shame, this one too was taught to me, by a junior in school at that. When I mentioned Amma's fellowship, Diptha had asked, 'She's going without you? Girl, mothers can't go alone like that. My family would throw such a tantrum.'

She was the one that first brought to my attention just how hairy I was, so obviously I took everything Diptha said very, very seriously. She'd grabbed my arm and made a face: 'God! How much hair you have, girl?' I couldn't believe I'd been blind to it until that very second, but then at once a spell was broken. 'Your hand's ditto like a man's. Dark, thick hair also.'

All requests for body-hair removal were promptly rejected by Amma. *You're too young for this now, just too young.* When I protested that I had seen her sit in front of a mirror and pluck away obsessively at her chin, she shot back: 'So you do know that this is what your future holds. Why, oh, why do you want to start this early? Go be free!'

My mother had a column in those years, in a magazine that was circulated among a few hundred posh housewives. The week after I asked her why I was so hairy, she wrote in that kitty-party rag of hers: 'The older women in my family used powder to remove all moisture from their skin, before going ahead and plucking their hair out like savages, with their bare nails. While the slightly well-to-do used talcum powder, some others had at hand powdered red brick, which they also used to clean their teeth. For the rest there was always sacred ash. The women who came before me had no money to call their own, and what were they going to tell their husbands and fathers? I need money to help get rid of my beard. So, the ash from their prayer shelves or the stove was what they used. All this for what? For their men to give them dozens of children to nurse alone? Which is why, to any young woman that may be reading this, I say, keep your hair, everywhere. You owe it to your foremothers.'

Amma's little essay had enraged a loony to burn some copies of the magazine, and it was all over the news. She had apparently hurt his sentiments, and he dared her to make fun of religions she didn't belong to. After vandalising the publisher's house and the poor woman's tiny Reva car, he threatened to take legal action. The editor-in-chief issued an apology since Amma wouldn't, and took a stricter approach to her recipe- and recipe-lore-only rule; no more columns for Amma either. This little controversy caused Amma's books to sell more than they had ever done before. A new liberal darling was born, thanks to my hairy legs. Amma, giddy from all this attention, doubled down on her no Anne French, no waxing, no shaving, no bleaching rule for me. These bloody jobless offence-taking men.

'Who's going to see you now?' The question stuck to me like Anabond through those school years. I couldn't tell Amma that it was for that one idiot girl who'd made my hirsuteness her business, but I knew enough to ask, 'Why should I do it for anyone? Why can't I do it for me?'

She was on to me. 'Nice try.'

I didn't tell her a thing about any of my friends because she did not hesitate to use them against me. Even Shyama, whom she hated for no reason at all, like she were bitter gourd.

My first thought when I saw Shyama the day she joined our school was, *does this girl have breasts?* She'd confide in me later that she was old, old enough to be in high school, had missed a few years moving from

Sri Lanka to Madras. Miss Barton, our Anglo-Indian class teacher, who always wore those pastel frocks that stopped at her knees and was way more popular with the girls than her saree-clad colleagues, brought Shyama in with her.

'Get along now, dearie,' she said to me, and sent her off to my desk.

Despite our very blah grey uniform, Shyama managed to come to school looking good, and I wanted to look like that. Her uniform stopped a good inch above her knee, and her knee patch was not at all dark, her arms and legs had zero hair. I found her very pretty, she had this sunny smiley face. We were the same height, so Shyama sat by me. Which gave me the opportunity to see just how effortlessly glam she was. Even the story of her name was glamourous: her dad fell so in love with the songs of *Aar Paar* he'd heard on Radio Ceylon, that he named her after the heroine of the film.

Soon enough I began imitating her, not everything all at once, because if someone (by someone I mean Diptha) called me a walking clone of hers that would've been too embarrassing. Amma, unprovoked, asked me to stay away from Shyama, *seems too precocious*. The way she said this made it obvious that Amma thought Shyama was taking up too much space in my life. Amma was busy being the heroine in her own story, but she couldn't stand Shyama's main character energy rubbing off on me. I stopped telling Amma anything about her then.

I visited Shyama's house after school often, without Amma ever catching a whiff of it. The first time I saw it, I was bowled over by her little house—it was smaller than ours but seemed way classier to me. There were lace doilies on her dining table (ours had Gelusil!). Her tall, movie-hero-type older brothers were listening to music in their squeaky-clean room; a large Michael Jackson poster surveyed them with a smouldering look. Her Mummy wore a floral skirt with a black top and had on these beautiful golden hoop earrings; her grandmother was in a yellow cotton midi dress. The two were at the table, bantering away loudly, a cheerful, comfortable domestic scene, the likes of which I'd only seen in those arthouse films Amma dragged us to sometimes. A solemn prayer wall with Mother Mary, Jesus on a cross and a brass candelabra led to the backyard, where their young cook was gutting fish. The house had a very different vibe: calm, sophisticated, like they knew how to live and weren't suffocating.

The first time I went there was because Shyama wanted to show me her stationery collection: she had a bag full of scented erasers and floral-scented ball-point pens, and I was obsessed with all things scented and glittery in those years. Some surly sisters loved to confiscate anything remotely cute-looking in school, so she didn't bring them to school.

She was left-handed and wrote beautifully, deliberately. We spent hours making greeting cards after school in her room. She taught me to dot my 'i' with a heart or a little circle that first day.

For my birthday that year, Shyama who, like any respectable elder, passed on her stationery to me, gave me a journal. I loved scrapbooking and spent most of my time at home cutting out pictures of whatever caught my fancy: a movie still with an action hero I liked, a landscape photograph, prints of popular paintings. I glued them on to the pages of my notebook, sometimes I copied the headline from the newspaper that came with it, at other times I wrote my own embarrassing titles. Since I already had a scrapbook that was fat with all those pictures, Amma suggested I use my fancy journal to record my dreams, *all the big writers do it.* Did she want me to be a writer, or was it her sneaky way of seeing whatever was going on in her problem child's problematic brain?

It was so damn pretty, only Shyama could have picked out that notebook, with its delicate blue and green flowers running around the pages. My scrapbook was just a rough notebook with ruled pages, an old book with leftover sheets from my previous school year, hardbound, with a drab light blue cover that had a black-and-white photo of a statue of Mother Mary.

I enjoyed not only writing my dreams down on this sickly-sweet girlie book, but also reading them out to Shyama. That was a big mistake. Big.

I must have been in some rice-induced coma when I had that dream about my friend Uma. That morning, I'd played with the neighbourhood minions, rode the Streetcat around the gullies that wound endlessly by our home, pigged out on rice and potatoes, and lay in bed listening to music on the Walkman, and eventually dozed off.

In my dream, buck-toothed Uma who lived on the third floor and I rode our cycles together, side by side, like friends in movies do, bonding over our super dark body hair, and the two plaits that hung around our faces like floppy dog-ears. We both rode boys' bicycles and were too tall for our own good and our age. A real bright morning in my dream, a sticky as hell day, and Uma was in a green skirt-blouse. I don't remember how she fell from her balcony, but the one grotesque thing I do remember from that dream is that she fell splat on the road, her face shattered, and in a blink, eight hangry mongrels surrounded her. They mauled dead Uma, and she just lay there like Krishna's Butter Ball in Mahabalipuram, like she was a rock superglued to the floor.

I couldn't bring myself to see her after this dream, the thought of seeing her made me want to weep. She called on the landline and even came to see me twice. I begged Amma to make up an excuse, pretended I had loose motions even. I didn't go out to play with anyone for a while actually, and that girl, Uma, she went and found new friends.

When Shyama called that week, Amma picked up the cordless in her room seconds before I could get to it. I overheard from the parallel line, hand over receiver so she didn't hear my breathing, as she interrogated Shyama. She wanted to know just what the beef between Uma and me was. Cunning Amma knew she could kill two birds with one stone; she could confront me about confiding in Shyama despite her strict instructions and she could snoop on my non-tiff with Uma.

Shyama, I didn't know this then, was freakishly close to her mother. She was actually friends with her mum and told her everything. The girl thought she would treat my mother like she too was my friend, which she decidedly wasn't then and never has been, and told her it was such a silly thing my imaginary cold war over a dream.

Amma then obviously asked to read my journal with all the gory details and then ran out and bought a book to understand her crazy child. Some book about psychoanalysing children's dreams.

In her head, the dream was somehow my doing, she acted like I had actually pushed Uma to her death and set the dogs on her. I had to stop talking to Shyama after that. Would you blame me? I didn't know how to deal with this weirdo who thought my mother was my friend.

At this point, when Amma was already wary of me, she caught Uma's sister and me with porn. Then she began to sound positively scared of me. The porn thing wasn't all that big a deal, but that was the thing that pushed my mother over the edge. After that, she was always jittery around me.

I had a lot of time at home in the summers before personal computers and Road Rash found me, so it was in the summers that I snooped in earnest. I would lock the door to a room at home and pick through a cupboard. I first went through my mother's things, found fifty chiffon sarees on the shelves, a few dozen blouses, bras and a few in-skirts. I was a wee bit scared to open the locker, which was a no-go zone, I wanted to, but I decided to go back to it later. I then went through my father's cupboard, it was as dull as him, files and files, with bills and papers. More papers. More files. More bills. Bell bottom trousers. Checked shirts. No locker. No cash. Nothing. I knew my parents shared the locker in my mother's cupboard, so going through his was a waste of my time.

When I got to Guru's wooden cupboard on the third day of May, I finally hit gold. A single, large pornographic poster, hidden between his clothes; bingo! He wasn't even being careful, the fool. It was almost as if the boy wanted to get caught. I picked the sheet out carefully, went to the other room, switched on the fan, drew the curtains and sat in bed like I was preparing for a quiz.

There was no dressing table in our house, nor any kind of full-sized mirror. So I went to the bathroom, removed the only mirror we had and planted it on the bed, by the headboard.

I obviously couldn't see my entire self in that tiny thing that my dad used to trim his moustache. I went part by part. First the face. 'Riddled by pimples and hair, an oily lump.' I got lipstick in my teeth and powder on my eyebrows and looked nothing like those models. By this point I had become conscious of just how thick and untrimmed my eyebrows were (thanks to Shyama and her beautifully arched, tamed eyebrows), I also had a not-so-thin moustache. 'I have sideburns!' Flab-less stick of a girl, I was not ever planning on showing my naked body to others. I was shocked to see myself, to see what every little part of me looked like at first. So alien to me, my own self. But after ten minutes, there was nothing left to stare at, I was . . . bored? I took one brief look at my form, front, back, the sides, the phantom curves, the place between my legs that had been disappointing in its entirety, the back of my legs, before returning the mirror to its place.

I went out to scout for someone, anyone. I *had* to tell someone, anyone. Priya, Uma's older sister, was out wearing that bored and lazy look that defined my childhood, one that I only ever saw on my kids' faces when their iPads were out of charge on a long flight.

'Why are you back so early from vacation?'

'My grandmother died.'

I then noticed the many pairs of slippers outside her house.

'I haven't been crying much. I was never close to her. Uma was,' Priya said.

Death could be this casual? What a star she was. I considered Priya briefly then, who looked like Uma, just a big longer and felt a special sort of respect for her.

'It will hit you soon. It hasn't sunk in. That's why,' I tried to explain.

Priya shrugged.

'Want to come to my house? I will show you something.'

She explained that she was not allowed there, they were a household in mourning.

'Meet me on the terrace in two minutes.' I wasn't giving up.

It was one. I didn't know where my mother was gallivanting or when she would come back wearing that suspicious look of hers. I stuffed the poster as carefully as I could into my new, unwieldy, impractical, ridiculously stylish denim drawstring school bag. I wanted to shock Priya. Wanted her to feel the same raw tremors I felt first when I saw the poster.

'Ready aa?' With the flourish of a magician pulling an endless ribbon out of his empty palm, I pulled the poster out.

'Eeewww!' Exactly what I wanted to hear.

I immediately collected the naked memorabilia, and sat on it so she couldn't see a thing.

'What is this?' Priya asked.

'Why do you want to see this?'

Priya was agitated, 'Show it to me. Show it now.'

We found ourselves on the parapet, our mouths wide open, giggling, exchanging notes.

'Mine is not this colour . . . ' Priya was pointing to the blonde's nipples when we heard the rustling.

I tried to push the thing into my stupid bag, but the strings just wouldn't open.

'What the fuck?' Guru's porn, Amma's first expletives (that I'd heard), I remember wondering what other monumental events awaited me that summer.

'This is not mine . . . This is not mine,' I'd screamed as Amma held me by the ears.

Priya, an alarmed cat, jumped and dashed out. Then she buried herself, rather conveniently, in that mourning hole of hers. Guru felt the sting of Amma's wrath, my cheeks burned too, both our ears had turned red from her deranged pinching and dragging as she screamed, speaking only in abuses. Amma was liquid rage, molten lava, and nothing would satisfy her until she made a bonfire in our backyard of the colourful lady. Seeing the naked body burn had made my stomach churn like I was at sea after a full meal.

I found myself wondering if that's what inspired Guru to make one of his own, a bonfire, not too long after. I didn't dare say it out loud ever.

That day Guru and I were made to hold each other's ears and squat, then stand up, while asking for forgiveness, over and over again. Guru didn't do more than five squats. He stormed out of the house, more out of embarrassment than anger.

'Like you are the epitome of honour.'

He slammed the door and ran up to the terrace while I busied myself with washing my 'filthy' school bag—that had to please her a bit even if she wouldn't admit it. Amma in the meantime made an SOS call to her friend, Waseem uncle. He was old and short, shorter than even me, and came home regularly to drive out the evil eye with resin and long peacock feathers. Amma believed in all kinds of spiritual mumbo jumbo—horoscopes, palmistry, gemstones, even tarot after she read something her hero Italo Calvino wrote. She had even been attempting to translate it because she couldn't find a Tamil version.

~

When I was around Amma during those growing-up years, it was as if an invisible chorus was singing shame-shame in my ears. Why did she want to be with my ultra-selfish dad? How did *he* get her to agree to be his second something, anything; what a gross, indecent arrangement! I felt bad for Amma sometimes (that was of course before I was forced to redirect all my feel-bad energies towards Guru).

My father now has enough money to be remembered as a jolly good man. He can give and give to his sons and me, and his former and current wife, and not have to worry about a damn thing. It came suddenly, this boom, and with it an immeasurable calm. It wasn't at all like this in my early years.

Immediately after Appa filed for divorce, the first wife began to show up at our home, and we'd all run helter-skelter because we knew it was about to get bad. She would make a loud scene out front, lashing out uncontrollably. Guru called it the belt treatment.

Once, when Amma wasn't around, and it was just Guru and me, she even sat at the entrance to our house with her minis—her sons really did look like miniature versions of her, not a trace of Appa—and warned the friends who'd come home to play with me: *Don't come to such homes; this is a brothel. Don't you know? Tell your mummies and daddies.*

~

I have had people tell me just *how* thrilling it must have been to have such a prolific writer-mother. To them I want to say (but never can for fear of it somehow reaching Amma): *Think of the worst things your mother has said to you, hopefully in private; mine has her characters say them in her books for all the world to see.*

My relationship with Amma had just begun to improve. I'd at long last left home for good. Amma had come to see me, and we were at a quiet restaurant eating lunch, and even spoke to each other like actual adult beings. Or so I thought. In a moment of weakness, I ended up telling her I was in therapy.

In her next novel, she got her revenge. Amma had her protagonist say:

If I were to give my children advice, especially my daughter, it would be to not have children. Why have these ingrates? You know being human is to make mistakes: grave and light. They make them a lot. Yet, you, the parent, especially the mother, seem to have been programmed to forget their follies, while they seem to need to spend a fortune on doctors, shrinks, astrologers, priests, whoever, to heal from the very idea of you. If you are the wound, mother, what then is even the point of mothering?

Despite this, I had to admit that it was easier being my sinning mother's daughter than it had ever been being saint Guru's sister. It was my grandmother, who first fashioned the minty fresh saint that was Guru.

He could do no wrong, her little scoundrel, top banana. Sometimes whole dishes would magically appear when Guru was at the table alone. Crunchy papads that my grandmother made from scratch, explosive chilli pickles with ladles of ghee, pieces of sweets she'd hidden in her floral handkerchief from the leaf meal she'd been served at whatever wedding or function she was attending. I suspected that she had somehow trained him to eat like a slow coach, to finish his meal last, so she could spoil him silly.

She never slapped him, not once, the way she did me for daring to clap back. Or yanked him out of a game or off his Streetcat for being out too late. Nor did she ever tie him up to a window like a dog like she did with me, because she thought I was incorrigible. (That's what my neighbour said, not like I remember being tied to a window like a dog as an eighteen-month-old). If she caught him doing things he shouldn't have been doing, the old woman simply cackled about it. No such concessions came my way. He could do no wrong, in her eyes. And I no right.

My mother had my absent father, Guru my ever-present grandmother, and all I had was this silly feeling that I was stranded, with no one to notice me. Dramatic I know, but what else is adolescence!

This was when I began to see us all not as a family, but as individuals (at least that's what my slightly overpaid shrink, who helped my little-girl self feel seen, thought). I rejected all invitations to join my family on their little outings when Amma forced Guru to wear his suspenders like he was some French mime. I refused to be seen with the likes of them.

I only made one exception, which was this bi-annual restaurant trip with my father. (This girl likes to eat, even if she doesn't like her family.) And my father, he had impeccable taste; rooftop tandoors where crackling naans would be dispensed hot off the oven, roadside dosas with burn-a-hole-in-your-tongue chutneys, hakka noodles from the boot of a van . . . he treated us to insanely good food when he finally showed up at home. That's where I drew my Lakshman Rekha. I didn't go to weddings, I didn't go to temples, I didn't go to Amma's book events, I didn't go anywhere that involved presenting myself as a part of them. I let my anger out in remarkably controlled measures, hiding someone's glasses, the other's keys, a third's purse. Scratching someone out of the photo album—especially cathartic. I'd use a divider, compass or a ball-point pen and go at it until their faces disappeared from the photo, and in its place remained just the white backing paper.

I never asked them for anything. Nor did they of me. And what could I give them anyway? It's because I had nothing from them that their time with me was so precious to me as a child. Even that began to slip away as I grew up.

~

When my mother finally hung up the phone that day, a familiar feeling—a distant ache, a sense of doom—smacked me. And then a singular thought took over any brain space I had left from feeding and keeping alive my forever-hungry, threat-to-their-own-selves children: when my mother called Guru about her surgery, she must have gabbed about *his* time in the hospital, they would have, *must* have spoken about his accident in great detail.

I had come very close to blabbing to her some years ago.

I asked her once what I could to do to stop feeling guilty all the time, without really giving her any other detail. I wanted to test the waters first. Surprisingly, she was open to the idea of my not being perfect, as if she had been expecting, no, no, waiting for this conversation. She had advice ready to go.

'We must do for people what they ask us to do for the gods when we have wronged. Penance? Supplication? Atonement? With the honesty of our heart. Sometimes I write stories in which the people I have wronged are the heroes and I am the villain. You have to do what you can, then you have to wait for grace, for mercy.'

'I am an engineer, not a writer, Ma. Give me something I can work with here?'

'Nothing I say is good enough.' She was going to make this about herself, wasn't she?

'That's not . . . ' I had no more words. 'You won't get it.'

Startled a bit by the stiffness of my tone, she finally conceded, 'You can confess.'

I was quiet.

'There must be a trial, before there can be pardon.'

Still not a word.

'You know . . . ' She was just going to tell me a story, I was relieved. 'I read that the ancient Greeks were all about mistakes that mortals made and punishments the gods gave them, but then slowly the gods, they seemed to evolve. They became less rigid. Now, we have gods with compassion, gods that forgive, prayers for sinners.' She paused.

I wanted to ask her: do you ever, like, feel unwell from guilt?

'I don't know,' she said, as if she heard me, so I'm not sure if I actually asked her or not.

I guess I'd just have to take it with me to my grave, at least that's what I think she meant.

I feel like such a different human now, I simply do not recognise the kid I was, a wildling. Amma said I had trouble, I caused trouble, I was trouble. Poor woman, I feel for her, I do. I was secretive and vengeful, both of which I could blame on my age, but even by the measure of childhood secretiveness and vengefulness, I was a bit much.

I'd fired more than one therapist for telling me I was okay, and would be okay, I needed to trust myself more, and that I didn't need to see them so often.

How could I be okay after what I did to him?

Amma asked me for the million-teenth time what I did after she went off to the hospital to admit Guru. I'd never been able to tell her; how could I, when Amma has never ever mentioned his name, never had a weak moment, unlike me, in all these years. It's as if the name Dileep fell off her mouth and crashed into a thousand pieces that day, and she'd never been able to scoop it all up, piece it back together and say it to me.

At first, she looked so tired and fragile, I thought she would break, and so I began to taunt her. I would come close to saying that name in front of my father, but change it to something else, and then start whistling like a fool. I would even break into songs that began with the 'Di' sound. But then it was no fun anymore because Amma stopped looking desperate. It was as if someone had turned off a switch, she became brazen again. Her old self. Her authoritative mother self.

The only thing I didn't know, but wanted to, was if that asshole Dileep had told her what I had told him.

Did the woman actually know?

I didn't want to see his monkey face ever again, didn't want to run into him. I didn't even know his damn full name, and I dared not to ask anyone for it. Who would I ask anyway? So, I became supremely fixated on the one thing I did know. I must have looked up the name Dileep a thousand and eight times growing up. First in the Yellow Pages, and later in those seedy internet chat rooms, then the messengers, comment sections everywhere strewn with vile, violent garbage, on YouTube videos of cricket matches where South Asian fans always brought their spicy A game, under news articles on Rediff dot com.

The first time I accidentally read his name after my mother stopped reacting to my taunts, something like an electric shock passed through me. I'd just started pretending to like reading newspapers. I was scanning the City Pages for something that I might want to read, I'd seen Amma do it every day. She'd make approving noises at her coffee, and offer running commentary as she read the newspaper.

Chain-snatching one street away from here!

Chain-snatching late in the night. Eighty-year-old woman was walking alone, and the boys cut her neck along with the chain.

Chain-snatching in train window seat. They cut off someone's ring finger and took their ring too!

On the days there had been chain-snatching anywhere near the city, she was both excited and worried. On those days, she reminded me of the hectic moon-game I played as a child. A bunch of us, five-year-olds, gathered in the late evening, and ran in completely different directions from our home, each of us screaming that the moon was chasing us. We would all gather later to freak out about how it had chased so many of us. Something about those chain-snatchings seemed to trigger Amma. She then scandalised us all by taking off her wedding chain like she was widowed whenever she went out late. On national holidays, she would do this even during the day because the streets were deserted. She made me take off my gilt earrings too.

The snatchers won't know it's fake. What if they attack you?

Amma loved to read the obits too. She liked to call people to let them know someone they knew had died. *Did you see?* She gathered a crowd and liked to go to these deaths.

So when I began reading the papers, I naturally gravitated to chain-snatching and related deaths.

I was reading a news item out loud one day when . . . I had to stop because a frog lodged itself in my throat.

Inspector Dileep said that a gang of three men in their early twenties had marked several women in the area as their targets, having tailed them for weeks. Police request women to be careful while walking alone in the streets.

I read that line, folded the paper back, ran into the toilet, and even though I hated how it always stank no matter what we washed it with, I locked myself up. I tore up the paper and threw it in the trash. In that weak moment, I also convinced myself that the Dileep I met, Amma's 'friend' Dileep, was this police inspector. Why else would she be so obsessed with chain snatchers?

Even if there was no way for me to verify the truth of this idea, that this man could be a cop was horrifying to little me.

Some friends and I were watching the San Diego Zoo video that everyone was talking about in college. This young, cute Jawed Karim in front of elephants, talking about their cool, long trunks; all of us talking about just how cute he was. So young and he had created YouTube; we were only fit for eating samosas, would never be creators of a damn thing. We were eating, laughing, talking and reading comments when all the laughter was knocked out of me. The username 'dileep0224' caught my eye, with a comment that simply said, 'you're a hero, soon to be millionaire. it's 6 pm.'

There were too many Dileeps on too many online forums, and each of them ugly and abrasive. I saw him even when I was not looking. There was a Google review for Dollops in Manipal from a Dileep S., and then I stopped going there, forever giving up those fat, fat spring rolls and Pepsi float that I so, so loved.

Amma, in one of her grand, ritualistic phases, told me that if I wanted to banish someone from my life, I had to tell them off, then have a hot water bucket bath with plenty of rock salt mixed in, and then, she said, I had to write their name in black ink on a piece of paper and say, *I thank you for the lesson you have taught me in this lifetime. Please leave me.* You burn the paper with their name and flush the ashes down the toilet. *Then you cleanse your aura with whatever you hold sacred.* I had laughed until I collapsed with hiccups when she said this, but late one night when I couldn't sleep, I did it all anyway. Except for the aura cleansing, I wasn't that far gone.

Amma had banished a lady who left a horrendous review for a short story collection, calling it a product of mediocrity in her obscure book blog.

~

I knew of my family's not-so-delicate predicament from a young age, that we weren't like others, that we were weird, but that we were all immoral. I only figured out what was different about us a little later, from the not-so-quiet whispers and the shame-laced taunts I heard between my parents when they fought, which was rare. Bit by tiny bit, I began to piece together the story of how my father was the originator of this group's shame.

Shame that would make Guru swear he'd never marry. He was still an impressionable teen then, but his logic seemed ironclad: some girl he loved would tell her parents that she wanted to marry him, they would (like normal Indian parents) inquire in their circles, or worse hire a family detective, and find out everything about him and his father's two families. They would say, *like father, like son, who knows he might do the same to our girl*, and then they would either forever have the upper hand, pestering him for details of events that happened before he was even an idea or an atom, or force the girl to call off the wedding.

This paranoia was fed to him by Amma herself one day as a semi-joke and a semi-taunt aimed at my father, though she liked to pretend that he wasn't married because of his accident.

It wasn't true because just a few years after the accident, when I was looking through Guru's cupboard, I found corny, cheesy poetry, beautiful love poems, clearly meant for a girl in his class. I had new respect for him then. I'd learned enough from my previous discovery, and didn't show this off to any of my silly gal pals who might blab to Amma.

It's what led me to a boyfriend in high school. To think I married my childhood sweetheart because of Guru's poetry sounds silly now, but it had had a maddening effect on me then. I was a profound copycat, a petty cat, who had to know that she could do everything he could.

Varun and I got together one day in school when he told me I looked a little bit like a model. I gave myself a fringe in the hope that he'd notice—and ding ding ding!

I was so different from them, the rest of my family, when it came to marriage—what with two small-town sons being raised in the hills, a lush wild garden that was visited by hummingbirds on most mornings, often I spotted dolphins in the ocean with Varun's hands in mine. That my path had swerved so far away from theirs, on to this stable track, made me check in often. Was I sane, was I really doing okay? I could never shake off the feeling that a bout of insanity was just around the corner and, when it came, it would be swift.

~

Growing up, everything about Amma felt suspicious. I was a very convincing conspiracy theorist (I was often my only audience). So, I kept one eye on her always, half expecting her to announce one day that she too had another family or child, or that she intended to, or that she was in the family way. If she smiled at some thoughtful boy-man for letting her skip ahead of him in a billing queue, if she giggled at a flat joke a friend's father cracked when he came to pick her up from home, if a distant relative who was staying with us was gossiping in the kitchen with my mother, because that's where she always gossiped, I lingered, heard every word she said.

I couldn't handle the idea of another family that I had to share with another parent. I wanted one that was mine and Guru's only, and in those years I acted like Amma was a dummy I owned, whose movements I could control, whose words would come from my mind like I were a ventriloquist.

'Do you expect me to act like an angry mutt whenever I meet a man?' she asked me once when I told her to stop embarrassing me. She'd cackled like a witch in front of a teacher we'd run into at a temple to which she had dragged me with the bribe of a crisp twenty-rupee note.

'You certainly have no trouble at all acting like that with your children.'

'Shut up or—' She left the threat unfinished because she wasn't her mother, she wouldn't hit us.

'Or?'

'Or I'll come to your school during the assembly session tomorrow, and I'll tell your entire school just what a filthy mind you have and how you denigrate your mother.'

My writer mother, words were the only assault weapons she needed, and something in the way she issued that threat made me very afraid. It felt like she might actually do it, so I immediately shrank back.

So, not even a week later, when I actually caught Amma crimson-handed in a near-embrace with Dileep, I was so angry I thought my eyes might pop.

The first time she shooed me away from the kitchen that day, I went and quietly scratched her out of a family photo. I wanted to take a second peek, just out of curiosity, so I went back into the kitchen making a big entrance when Dileep's creepy crawly arms were over my mother's shoulders, his hairy fingers on her back.

I slammed the kitchen door, and then I latched the damn thing tight with as much power as I could muster, like I was at a hand pump, drawing water, jumping up and down. That's when I heard the noise. Guru was on fire.

If I had gone to him and rolled him on the floor then, like they had taught us to in the fire drill at school, he would have been perfectly fine, but my legs became trunks planted firmly in the yard, like the coconut and guava I tended to every evening.

Amma whisked Guru away. Dileep handed me over to a neighbour.

He was about to leave when something like a fever came upon me, and I vomited the words, 'I latched the door from the outside.'

He pulled his hand away—hairy, but also surprisingly soft—and took a step back. No words. Then I saw it, or I thought I saw it, even if only for a teeny tiny moment, something close to revulsion crossed his eyes.

4

And After

Everyone else returned from a visit home with masalas, pickles and papads, but my parents deemed it fit to send me away with things they no longer needed. They were too old school to give stuff away to the housekeeper, and forget about throwing away things that did not work, they'd rather it just sat on their dusty showcase. They could only stomach giving these worthless baubles to Aparna and me. So, on the last day of my yearly visit, every time, I have to choose between a showdown with them or extra luggage. Some years I leave in a huff. This year, I chose the baggage because I felt bad for my mother.

After weeks of keeping her company, of staring into my phone to avoid confrontation, of complaining on Zoom to friends who seemed to be running out of advice on keeping the peace with parents, I left. Amma and I got along fine at first. We managed to eat our meals together, drink evening tea, watch the night news bulletin on TV together, and were astonished to find that we agreed on things often. But we were too alike, and most days ended in a mini storm.

I packed another suitcase, and stuffed it with an ugly unframed painting my mother had received as a memento at some literary shindig, boxes of stale snacks, outdated gadgets, a torchlight that only worked when it was plugged in, a watch that couldn't be repaired and a two-kilo karlakattai shoulder club that my father had been conned into buying by his hipster gym coach.

When I got into the Uber and waved, they seemed smaller, and I somehow unfairly powerful. Fifteen years, that's all the time it had taken for this role reversal. Time had crept up on them, and then illness had robbed them of authority; what remained was some grown-up version of helplessness. I wondered how they felt just then, watching me leave.

I was on my way to a diving school along East Coast Road. They didn't know. I told them I was heading to the airport. It was originally my French-class mate Dheeran's idea. I'd run into him at a garden café while I was day-drinking out of sheer boredom. He had just completed an introductory diving course and wouldn't stop raving about this place outside town. His photos looked so good that I went home and booked myself a slot.

What was I thinking when I signed up? A few years ago, I had nearly capsized a boat while snorkelling. The instructor had told me to jump, and I did, hurtling into the open sea. Almost instantly, fear took over my being, a paralysing fear, the kind I hadn't known in years. Though

I wore a life jacket, I held on to a side of the boat, just unable to let go. The boat swung this side and that as I kicked, trying but failing to keep the water away from my eyes and nose.

My instructor tried in vain to get me to let go, to swim, but I wouldn't. I stayed there, bobbing up and down, coughing. When I began to wheeze, he finally accepted defeat and helped me back up onto the boat. I sat watching the others, even a seven-year-old, glide through the ocean like fish. I wasn't alone though. A man nearly my age didn't even attempt the jump. He sent his wife and kid ahead, and then stayed back, watching me struggle. I wondered if he felt vindicated when I climbed back up, drenched. He was dry and cool, whistling.

After a minute or so he said, 'My wife wants to be brave, because she doesn't want my son growing up like . . . well, like us, you know?'

I nodded.

'My mother was always afraid something would happen to me. Anytime I wanted to do something even slightly adventurous, her first reaction was—*Ayyo no. Careful pa.*' His voice rose, mimicking her fluster.

'Maybe we were better off a generation ago. Back then, they all had nine, ten children and let them run wild. But our parents, they only had two. They lived in fear, terrified of the humiliation, the burden of dying after us.'

I realised it was my turn to speak.

'I had a burns injury as a kid. I don't think my mother ever got over it.' Between fifteen and twenty-two, when I finally left home, she raised me like a damsel in distress. I could no longer cycle to school, *what if a bus hits you?* No school trips, *what if there's an accident?* I couldn't even kiss a girl in peace until my twenties, Amma was always there, hovering, watching.

The conversation with a grown man about Amma's worries, and how her voice grew inside my head over the years, and then hearing him admit he was doing the same thing to his son, somehow, instead of unsettling me, calmed me. I felt less alone.

I told my parents I had a short layover in Delhi, and then it was home to Paris. I skipped over the specifics of my itinerary so I could make up facts when I needed to. When my cab arrived, I dumped my luggage in the dicky swiftly, and ducked out of home, waving goodbye, so the driver wouldn't accidentally tell them I was driving down the scenic beach road, not to the airport. In my hands, I had a spiral-bound copy of Amma's new book, one she hadn't even shown her editor yet. She wanted me to read it first.

I knew why. All through my stay, she had tried to reach out. But she wasn't a part of my present. It wasn't by design. I saw her in the rearview mirror. Necessary, distant. Now and then, we found something to reflect on together, but we did not have much to do with each other. When I visited, or occasionally when she visited me, we spoke, but it was never with the intensity of childhood. That surfaced only when she pushed me, when I lost control. Blinded by rage, saying things I couldn't stop, old neural pathways resuscitated.

Some years ago, she tried to convince me to work with her publisher. She wouldn't admit it, but I knew she found my work wanting. She never understood why I studied French, why I hadn't just gone to college for a degree. I knew she regretted showing me that Alliance Française building. We were walking back home from somewhere, when she said casually, 'I saw my first Rohmer here. They teach French. Sometimes they show movies.'

A school that showed movies appealed to me. I didn't know who Rohmer was then. By the time I joined the French course there, I had heard enough about him from Amma. I had time for a part-time job, as a radio jockey at a new private Tamil FM station. After wasting years on Organic Chemistry and Calculus, I was relieved to be working with languages.

After earning an advanced diploma at AF, I worked my way up the interpretation circuit. Then, unexpectedly, I reached Paris. There was no going back. All of it without so much as a pretence of help from my preoccupied parents.

My father's bridge-building business was unpredictable. In those years, we never knew if he would return on a business class flight or be deported like a prisoner. Which is why Amma raised us so that if we truly were to lose everything, it wouldn't feel any different. We knew how to take the bus and local train, we sat on the floor and ate, slept on the floor on a thin mattress. We knew to replant mint stalks, to grow drumstick and edible vines in the backyard in case we ever needed an urgent meal.

Unless it was a wedding, we didn't dress up, clothes were bought once a year. We wore Hawaii slippers. And none of us carried much money. When I started working, I learned slowly to live on my own money. But the thought that my father might leave us and return to his first family never did leave me. That's why I refused to go to college.

Amma was very unhappy about it all. But now clearly she thought that having a son who translated for a European publishing house was the perfect flex to impress her writer friends. She would kill two birds with one stone, prove her point about my worth, and in the process, win some white man's approval for her work. For a while, I pretended to be interested. Then I couldn't anymore. She handed me her new book, I suspected, to convince me to translate again, though never asked outright. *Just read it*, she said.

~

It wasn't overcast, that would have been perfect for the drive. Instead, it was a clear day, perfect for the dive. I felt both hopeful and panicked. Before doing anything that made me tingly with fear, I tried to picture myself overcoming it. In the sedan's back seat, I closed my eyes and saw myself underwater, calm as a fish. I saw myself on the boat after the dive, quiet, proud, like I was in a movie about rich young brats. *You did good, you did good*, I imagined telling myself, patting my own back.

I tried to go back to a time in my life when I was not afraid. Not of anything or anyone. I thought of a monsoon from my childhood. Rains that felt like the end of the world, our home drenched in darkness. My baby sister crying nonstop, she was of course scared. She didn't understand why our home was a jail we couldn't escape, why thunder pierced our windows and rattled the glass.

My mother fumbled through the darkness to find a kerosene lantern. But we ran out of kerosene soon, and there was no sign of power coming back. A cyclone was lashing the city. Amma brought out a brass lamp from the prayer room. She lit all five of its wicks and placed the lamp in the middle of the room. She sat up all night, fanning the baby with a day-old newspaper. She was worried, I could tell. She missed my grandmother then, this too I could tell. Was she rethinking her life with the man she shared with another woman, this I never could tell. Yet, none of that worried me. I was unafraid of the present, or the future. I knew everything would work out for me. It had to.

It was my grandmother who'd given me the strength to feel that way. And for a while after she died, I clung to that feeling. She helped me think the world was designed to work for me. She treated me like I was a man already, it was all I needed to feel like one.

Days after Amma came home with Aparna from the hospital, my grandmother summoned me to the kitchen, her tone officious. She handed me a whole ash gourd, heavy and smooth. I could barely hold it. She made me carry it to the living room, had me carve out a small square at the top. Then she passed a bag of vermillion, I had to pour it inside. With a knife, I mixed the insides of the gourd until only the shell was a mild green, everything within had turned red. She handed me eleven rupees in coins, which I pushed inside the gourd. She sat on the floor giving instructions, I sat next to her. I sealed the gourd with the square I had cut out, then carried it outside our threshold. She handed me a camphor to light atop the gourd. I moved it in slow circles, warding off the evil eye from my mother and newborn sister.

That she entrusted me with the gourd ritual meant something to me. That she had me prepare it, wield it like a weapon against evil, helped me feel reassured. I was the older brother. She taught me to be brave, sensing I had to learn it. When she died, I felt unmoored. I was supposed to have been the one to care for them all, but after my accident, I was the one being watched. The one that needed caring for. The one carried to the hospital, for whom the evil-eye-removal ritual was performed, some weeks with salt, some with resin, some with camphor, and at other times with sacred threads, red, black and yellow.

I had assumed my sister would always be my 'responsibility', a feeling that was strong for at least as long as my grandmother was alive. But sometime in my late teens, she drifted away. As adults, we tried to reconcile, but by then she had already reconciled with my father, and his fortune. That reunion was the main story of her life, of his—and my mother's, of course. I never could figure out how Amma and Aparna could simply embrace him when he finally made his money, when he started staying home instead of living elsewhere. Aparna wanted to stitch together an imaginary version of the four of us. She had already built her picture-perfect family with Varun. She didn't really need one more.

I ignored Aparna's invitations and dismissed her offers to visit. I also left Chennai every year before she could make it there. This year, though, it did seem like she had had enough, she didn't come even when I called, when I wanted a break.

My own relationship with my father wasn't particularly strained. We were as close as he wanted us to be. He'd spent most of my visit staring at his phone, shut away in his room, or leaning over his laptop. Occasionally, he asked if I had money to invest in some scheme. I declined politely. We made small talk. Watched a cricket match or two. More than once, when I watched him struggle up the stairs, I felt bad for him. He didn't seem to be in great shape. The thought of his mortality crossed my mind on those days. The possibility that, one day, I'd have to visit home to care for him. I shrugged it off. I wasn't his only son. I wasn't his first. It wouldn't fall on me.

A song from my childhood played on the radio, a guitar-heavy composition I had once been obsessed with. The cab moved through familiar streets, empty and quiet on this Sunday morning, until we reached the mouth of East Coast Road. The city had stretched farther south, and its biriyani shops had reached farther down the beach road. Once-sleepy hamlets had turned into posh neighbourhoods with beach-view villas. The arterial road felt narrower now, choked by petty shops, places of worship, endless eateries. It took us a while to get out of there, and then, all too suddenly, the road widened, traffic thinned.

I opened Amma's new book. The first page had a prose poem titled *Oru Thalai Kadhal*. One-sided love. I read it and returned the book to my backpack, zipped it closed. I asked the driver to turn up the radio.

At the hotel, I checked into my room, then walked down to the diving school. I got there feeling a bit relaxed. In the locker room, I changed into a wetsuit, watching myself in a mirror. Then I caught the trainer's gaze linger over my scars. I didn't mind them, the scars. It was just skin, bumpy, white here, dark there, like light and shadow. And yet, when someone noticed it, I felt the need to quickly cover up and explain. Worried they'd mistake it for something contagious. They wouldn't want me in the pool if they thought it was contagious, would they?

I considered what to tell the instructor as I struggled into my tight suit. Then I sat down on the locker room bench, and told her everything. She listened, bewildered, her mouth slightly open.

'The good thing about this place is, we don't leave anything to chance,' she said. And then some more reassurances: *You're here to explore the water safely with us. You're in good hands. You need only think about that and have yourself a good vacation.*

Then she said, 'My aunt had a fire accident too, many years ago. She has two kids now.'

I looked at her then. She was at least half a decade older than me.

'I am glad your aunt is okay.'

At the practice session in the pool, I did terribly. When the instructor took the guard from my mouth, I panicked, flailed my arms and swam up to the surface. I thought she might send me, the bad candidate, away. But she only looked at me, slightly bemused.

'It happens to most adults. Children handle this better. You'll be fine, let's try again,' she said.

'Are we going into the ocean today?' I was not ready, I knew.

She nodded yes.

I went back under and did my best to not panic. After about twenty minutes, I thought she'd given up.

But she said, 'We will try directly in the ocean, that might be better.'

We walked up the beach, past fishing nets, to the waiting catamaran. Others were already seated, all suited up. Even a little girl.

The foaming ocean reminded me of something a woman once said about my scars. Every woman I'd been with had tried to make something of the scars, as if she needed a reason to justify this desire for a mutilated body. Always searching for beauty, invariably reaching for a trite metaphor.

One called my scars milk and froth. Another, the salty foam of the ocean, she even bent down to lick it. A third likened them to the inundated landscapes of the moon. I had to try hard not to laugh that day.

I hadn't met anyone who had been as casual about it as this instructor. She didn't feel the need to react to my story. Or valorise the scars.

It was an accident. Just an accident. That's all it was.

True, if it hadn't happened, some scar-less version of me would be going diving. But this version was here now. Who's to say which one I'd prefer if I met them both today?

The other instructor, a young man, stood at the edge of the catamaran, dropped the anchor, then sent his candidates flopping backwards into the middle of the ocean, one by one. They fell unquestioningly, like dodos in an animation film.

I watched, trying to stay calm. But already I could already feel the bile rising to my ears.

The young instructor came over and quietly got me ready. My own instructor didn't even look my way. She knew I was scared. Instead, she jumped into the sea, and helped the others stay afloat.

'Ready?' he asked, his hands firm on my sternum.

He had pricked a balloon. I'd deflated instantly, exhaling loudly.

'Nothing's going to happen. See all these people? You will go in and come right back out.' Poor guy must be sick and tired of us scaredy cats.

'I don't want to fall backwards,' I begged.

'You have to fall this way,' he said mimicking the motion. 'That way, you'll float on your back.'

'Wait.'

I took my phone out.

I wasn't going to earn my mother a thing. Not money. Not fame. Her translations wouldn't do well. But the woman I had to meet to fail at all this, the publishing assistant Prashanti, was, according to my mother, *the stuff of magic*. 'She's waiting for your call.'

I saw them then—fish jumping like popcorn in the ocean, happy levitating rascals.

I didn't know about Amma, but *I* was due some magic.

I messaged her. 'Send me this Prashanti's number.'

And then I jumped.

One-sided Love

Thangamey, you used to love me, you just don't remember. Your eyes lit up when I entered a room, your smile was aimed at me even in a crowd of blurry faces. You cried, then melted into sleep in my arms, curled like a comma, and for months, I slept with a comma on my lap. Whose fault is it that only I remember? Whose fault that something so precious lives only in my memory?

I want you to know, now that I may leave, that we had each other, even if briefly, and briefly it seemed to both of us, like that was all we needed.